What could *Tess do to help save Ms. M's wedding?*

"WHAT IS YOUR PROBLEM?" ERIN ASKED.

"Nothing," Tess called over her shoulder to Erin. But Tess walked faster toward the exit.

"Oh, yeah." Erin raced and caught Tess's arm just as they walked outside. "You always run away from me when nothing's wrong."

Tess shrugged Erin's hand off her arm. "Don't worry about it, okay? Do you still want me to wait with you until your mom comes?"

"You don't have to if you don't want to," Erin said.

Neither of them spoke for another minute or two. Then Tess sat down on the curb next to Erin. Tess wasn't exactly ready to walk out on her Secret Sister.

Erin chipped a scrap of yellow paint off the curb, peeling it back with her fingernail. "It's not like I offered to be the junior bridesmaid or anything."

Tess turned her head away from Erin. She snuffled. "I know. Once again you get to do something that I don't. It's not fair."

Secret Sisters: (se´-krit sis´-terz) n. Two friends who choose each other to be everything a real sister should be: loyal and loving. They share with and help each other no matter what!

Secret ✳ Sisters

Petal Power

Sandra Byrd

WaterBrook
PRESS

PETAL POWER
PUBLISHED BY WATERBROOK PRESS
5446 North Academy Boulevard, Suite 200
Colorado Springs, Colorado 80918
A division of Random House, Inc.

Scriptures in the Secret Sisters series are quoted from the
International Children's Bible, New Century Version,
copyright ©1986, 1988 by Word Publishing,
Dallas, Texas 75039. Used by permission.

The characters and events in this book are fictional,
and any resemblance to actual persons or events is coincidental.

ISBN 1-57856-115-9

Printed in the United States of America
1999—First Edition

10 9 8 7 6 5 4 3 2 1

For my beautiful and gifted sister, Sara Mike,
the best junior bridesmaid ever

one

Crying Her Eyes Out

Thursday, April 17

The squeaking of the girls' sneakers echoed off the locker-lined walls. The place looked more like a ghost town than an elementary school.

"Where are you dragging me?" Tess Thomas asked as her best friend tugged her by the arm down the empty hallway.

"Come with me, and I'll show you," Erin Janssen whispered back, tucking a runaway piece of caramel-colored hair back into her loose French braid. "I'm telling you, I heard crying. Loud crying. And I know it was Ms. Martinez."

"When we left her twenty minutes ago, she was fine," Tess insisted. She couldn't picture her sixth-grade teacher crying—not in school anyway. The hallway was hot. The school was hot. She wanted to go home and take a dip in the pool, not slither around the school after hours. Dots of sweat sprang out on her forehead, itching under her coffee-brown hair.

"Well, if you call bawling your eyes out fine, then she's fine. But I don't," Erin persisted.

Tess followed along but rolled her eyes as she flashed a lopsided smile at her best friend. Erin was not only her best friend but also her Secret Sister. And Secret Sisters did almost everything together, including after-school detective work.

To Tess's surprise, as they approached the end of the narrow hallway, she did hear crying. Sobbing, actually. And it came from their sixth-grade classroom. "You're right! It's her!"

"I told you," Erin said. "Should we go in? I mean, what if she wants some privacy?"

Tess stubbed the rubber toe of her shoe over and over again against the smooth concrete floor. "But what if we can help? It always makes me feel better to talk with someone."

The girls listened as Ms. M. blew her nose and then sniffed a little. "It sounds as if she's quieting down," Erin observed, turning to leave. Just then another wave of weeping began.

Tess, eyes wide as windows on a warm spring day, looked at Erin. "I think we'd better go in. Maybe we can help."

Erin nodded.

"Okay, here goes nothing." Tess turned the handle to the classroom door and pushed. The massive door's hinges wailed. The two girls tiptoed in, unsure of what they would find.

two

What Can I Do?

Thursday Afternoon, April 17

"Oh!" The creaking door must have startled Ms. M. As she looked up at the girls, the box of Kleenex slipped from her hand, clattering to the floor. She bent over to pick it up, and her thick black hair tumbled over her shoulders like a glossy river of nighttime. Then she sat up straight in her chair, looking more like their teacher again.

"Tess," she said, wiping a fast hand across her cheeks to erase the tear trails. "Erin."

"Um, hi," Tess started. What else could she say? Silent seconds ticked by; Tess picked at her hangnail nervously. Oh, why had they come in?

"We, uh, heard some crying. And my mom isn't going to be here for a few minutes, so we thought, you know…" Erin took a deep breath. "Maybe we could help?" she finished hopefully.

"Oh, girls." Ms. M. waved them to pull up two chairs beside her. "That's sweet; it really is. But I'm afraid there's nothing you, or anyone, can do at this point."

"You're still getting married, aren't you?" Tess blurted out, then clapped her hand over her mouth. What if the answer was no, and Tess had made Ms. M. start to cry all over again?

"Yes, I'm still getting married. Anthony is just as wonderful as ever."

"Anthony," Tess whispered. "What a dreamy name."

Erin elbowed Tess back to reality.

"Is something else wrong then?" Tess asked cautiously.

Ms. M. hesitated before answering. "It's just that Anthony's niece, Amber, was going to be my junior bridesmaid. It's been planned for months." Ms. M. looked at her fingers, twisting the engagement ring around and around. "And now, well, she's not." A fresh trickle of tears slipped from the corners of her eyes.

"She didn't die, did she?" Tess asked.

Elbowing her again, hard this time, Erin whispered, "Tess!"

"No." Ms. M. looked up, smiling gently. "In fact, it's something wonderful. She's had a bad disease for many years and has been waiting for a kidney transplant. Do you remember when we talked about transplants in science? That's one reason I was so interested in studying them. Now her name has come up on the list, and she's going to have one. Tomorrow."

"We remember what it is, I think," Erin said.

Ms. M. reminded them. "Her kidneys don't work anymore, so they transplant another one into Amber's body so she can be healthy again."

"Where do they get the kidney? I mean, is it a fake one?" Tess asked. This time Erin didn't elbow her.

"No, it's real. It came from another person—someone who died this morning. I just found out about it during lunch hour."

"Oh." Tess squirmed.

"Anyhow, I'm glad for her. I'm just a little worried, hoping that she'll pull through okay." Ms. M. sniffed.

"Is that it then? I mean, is there anything else?" Tess forged forward. Surely there was more to it than that.

"Well…" Ms. M. looked reluctant to continue. Then she whispered so softly the girls could barely hear her. "And something else, but it's silly."

"What did you say?" Tess scooted her chair closer to Ms. M.'s big wooden desk. Erin scooted her chair closer, too, the metal feet scratching the tile floor as she did.

"It's so silly I don't even want to say anything about it. I mean, in light of all the good this operation is going to do," Ms. M. said, her voice as soft as kitten fur rubbing the back of your hand.

"We won't think it's silly," Erin offered.

"Right!" Tess said. "We promise." She leaned closer and smiled at her teacher to let her know they understood. "One time I was sad because my mom threw away my old shoes. My brother thought that was dumb, but Erin understood. Girls do that." She smiled.

"Well, Amber's mother and father don't have enough money to cover the surgery costs. So all the relatives are pitching in." Ms. M. swallowed hard. "Including Anthony and me. We decided this afternoon."

"That was really sweet!" Tess said. But as she saw tears flood Ms. M.'s eyes again, she knew she had said the wrong thing. Again. She moved slightly away from Erin, avoiding another possible elbow jab.

"But there's still not enough money for Amber's surgery, right? That's why you're upset." Tess tried again to say the right thing.

"No, no, there's enough." Ms. M. sighed.

"What then?" Erin asked. "Anthony wants to delay the wedding?"

"No," Ms. M. said.

"You can't celebrate when she's sick? You can't have a reception?" Tess guessed.

"Of course we can celebrate. She's getting well. And yes, we'll have a reception. It's all paid for…almost." The last word slipped out reluctantly. Ms. M. looked as if she would like to take it back.

"What isn't paid for?" Tess forged ahead. She wanted this wedding to be perfect. It had to be. Ms. M. deserved it.

"Well, flowers for one. And the other is…um…" Ms. M. dabbed her eyes. "No honeymoon."

"No honeymoon!" both girls cried at once.

"Oh, I'm so sorry," Erin said. "Did you have it all planned and everything?"

"Yes." A dreamy look shadowed Ms. M.'s eyes, and she looked above their heads and beyond them as she continued. "We love nature. You know, Anthony is a science teacher." She smiled at the sound of his name. "We wanted to go somewhere close. So we planned a trip that was very special, just right for us. Three days at the Red Rocks Resort in Sedona. Hiking among the Red Rocks, just the two of us, wading barefoot in the creek, breathing the clear spring air. Meadow picnics. Dining outside at night by candlelight, just the two of us."

She looked at the girls. "You know, my parents never had a honeymoon. So my mom helped me plan this one. She's just as excited as Anthony and I are. I mean, she was." Ms. M. sniffed again, dabbing her nose with a crumpled tissue. "But I guess it'll be all right. We'll just stay home. We can always go another time."

Now what could Tess say to that? Nothing. A vacation later wasn't a honeymoon. Poor Ms. M.! And Ms. M.'s mother and Anthony. What a mess.

Neither girl said a word.

"Here's a picture of Amber." Ms. M. opened her desk drawer and showed it to the girls. "She's a lovely girl, and I'm so glad for her." A cool breeze floated through the room's open window, swirling through the stuffy air.

Ms. M. must have felt it, too, because she moved toward the window to open it wider.

Amber was a pretty girl. "What can we do?" Tess whispered to Erin. "We have to help her somehow!"

Erin shrugged her shoulders. She didn't have a chance to say anything before Ms. M. sat back down.

Tess stood up, ready to hand the picture to Ms. M., when a thought struck her. She couldn't do anything about the honeymoon or the flowers, but she could help out as a junior bridesmaid. It would be perfect, and Tess would love to be in the wedding.

Tess opened her mouth to suggest her fabulous plan, but just as she did, Ms. Martinez spoke up. "Oh! You know what? I just had a thought!" She stood up. "Erin, come here."

Erin walked over to Ms. Martinez, and she turned Erin around, looking at her from all angles.

"Yes, yes, it just might work." Ms. M. beamed. "Erin, would you like to be the junior bridesmaid? You're just about the same size as Amber. She has nice long legs like you and is slender, too."

"Me?" Erin smiled. "What do I have to do? I don't have to stand up front or anything, do I?"

"Well," Ms. M. said with a smile, "I had planned for her to stand up front with the rest of us. Also, she is, I mean, she was, going to hand out the packets of birdseed to the wedding guests to toss as we leave the church. We were going to have rose petals, to match the rest of the wedding flowers." A slight frown shadowed her pretty face. "But not anymore."

"Well, okay. I'll do it," Erin said.

Tess understood Erin's struggle. She didn't like to be in front of a lot of people. But Tess didn't mind. Then again, Ms. M. hadn't asked Tess.

Erin beamed at Tess. Tess, however, did not beam back.

"Can you come for a fitting next Thursday night? Do you think your parents will agree?" Ms. M. grinned, joy shining in her eyes—the first joy Tess had seen since they had started talking with her this afternoon. The whole situation curdled the milk in Tess's stomach. This was her plan; Erin hadn't even thought of the idea!

"I'm sure they wouldn't mind. And I'd love it!"

Ms. M. turned toward Tess. "You don't mind, do you, Tess? You'll still be at the wedding with the rest of the class."

"I think Erin will make a great junior bridesmaid." But her words were flat. Erin was her Secret Sister, the one Tess would turn to in time of trouble. But she hadn't counted on this.

Tess picked up her backpack and said, "We had better get going. Your mom's probably waiting for you outside, and I need to get home."

"Yeah, I guess." Erin looked inquiringly at Tess.

"Thanks. I'll call your parents tonight." Ms. M. smiled at Erin, then gave both girls a hug. "I hadn't meant to tell you two all that. However, since I did, I appreciate your kind hearts and ears."

"It was nothing," Tess said. At least in her case it was nothing. She hadn't done anything to help, and it didn't look like she was going to.

They stepped out into the hall, and Tess walked quickly to stay a few steps ahead of Erin. This wasn't Erin's fault, Tess knew, but she still felt steamed. Better to get home, and fast.

"Wait up, would you?" Erin called. "What is your problem?"

three

A Plan

Thursday Afternoon, April 17

"Nothing," Tess called over her shoulder to Erin. But Tess walked faster toward the exit.

"Oh yeah." Erin raced and caught Tess's arm just as they walked outside. "You always run away from me when nothing's wrong."

Tess shrugged Erin's hand off her arm. "Don't worry about it, okay? Do you still want me to wait with you until your mom comes?"

"You don't have to if you don't want to," Erin said.

Neither of them spoke for another minute or two. Then Tess sat down on the curb next to Erin. Tess wasn't exactly ready to walk out on her Secret Sister.

Erin chipped a scrap of yellow paint off the curb, peeling it back with her fingernail. "It's not like I offered to be the junior bridesmaid or anything."

Tess turned her head away from Erin. She snuffled. "I know. Once again you get to do something that I don't. It's not fair."

"What are you talking about?" Erin moved to the other side

of Tess. Now they looked at each other. "We almost always do things together. Sometimes I pick them, sometimes you do. Like spring break. You planned that whole trip."

In spite of herself Tess smiled. That was true; she had arranged their vacation together last month. It was a total blast.

"I guess. It's just that I really want to do something to help Ms. M. And it's not like I can buy her flowers or pay for a honeymoon."

"Why not? What happened to 'Tess to the Rescue'?" Erin teased.

"I'm fresh out of rescue ideas." Tess fiddled with the straps on her backpack. She guessed it would be okay just to go to the wedding with everyone else. She could still ride home with Erin. Trickles of sweat slid down the back of Tess's neck. She fanned herself with her open hand.

"Why don't you let me help you think of something?" Erin offered, smiling at her friend. "You're more than a friend; you're a sister." Each of them had only brothers— Tess had one and Erin had two. But each had always wanted a sister. So they chose each other to be sisters. They promised to stick by one another in everything and be loyal like no other friend would be. But Tess couldn't shake loose the disappointment.

"No thanks."

Neither of them spoke again for a few minutes.

Finally, Erin cleared her throat. This time she looked away from Tess, staring over the almost-empty schoolyard. "You know, it seems like you always want to help me, with spring break or my homework or whatever. You never think I can help you." Erin's voice rose a little. "Do you think you're better than me?"

Tess whipped her head around. "How could you think that? I don't think I'm better than you. It's just…it's just…" *It's just what?* she wondered. She really didn't know.

"Well, you have to let other people help you sometimes, too." Erin said.

Tess flung her arm around her pal. "You're right. I'm sorry I was being such a snob. Maybe we can come up with a plan together." This time *she* chipped yellow paint from the curb. "We don't have much time since Ms. M. is getting married in nine days. What can I do?"

"Well, we can't do anything about their trip, but maybe we can help with the flowers," Erin said.

They sat together, quiet in the still valley of afternoon. A swarm of baby bees whirled around them on the way to the bush next to Erin. Its mustard-yellow flowers drooped a little. Erin glanced at the flowers and leaped up.

"Why don't we ask all the kids to bring flowers?" Erin suggested.

"Nobody in Arizona has flowers in their yard. And if everybody brought them, they wouldn't go together. And they're expensive."

"If only we knew someone who owned a flower shop," Erin said. "You don't know anybody, do you?"

"I don't know," Tess answered. "My mom or dad might. Why?"

"Well, you could call them and ask them to donate flowers. Then at least Ms. M. will have flowers for her wedding. It just won't be a pretty wedding without flowers."

"I know. And I think Ms. M. thinks so, too, even though she's trying not to complain," Tess answered. She thought so hard a headache throbbed in her temples. She filed through her memory. Who owned a flower shop? There must be someone. Wait. Didn't her mom have a friend who did flowers?

A light voice lilted across the parking lot, and Tess snapped out of her thoughts.

"'Bye, girls. See you tomorrow," Ms. M. called out. She was smiling but still clutching the box of Kleenex.

"We have to think of something," Tess said. Just then Erin's mother pulled up, and Tess was glad. She wanted to run home as fast as she could to ask her mother if her friend possibly could help out. Tess didn't understand why, but she knew she must do something for Ms. M.'s wedding.

four

Discount Shopping

Thursday Afternoon, April 17

"Mom!" Tess ran into the house, banging the door shut. The windows rattled, and one of the pictures in the front entryway shook itself crooked at the force, but she didn't stop to fix it. She had a mission.

"And a big hello to you, too!" Her mother laughed as Tess ran into the kitchen. Tess's mother, Molly, set down the knife she was using to peel red potatoes. Her pregnant tummy rounded out, spacing her several inches away from the sink.

"I mean, 'Hi, Mom.' But also, you have to help me save Ms. Martinez's wedding!" Panting, Tess tossed her backpack on the floor and grabbed a paper cup. "Don't you know a florist?" she finished, pushing the water-cooler button to start a stream of cool water into her cup. After gulping for a minute, she looked at her mother expectantly.

"No, I don't think I do. I'm certain I don't. Why do you ask?"

"Oh." Tess crushed the paper cup and pitched it into the garbage. "Just great. What about your friend, uh…" Tess searched for her name. "Alice."

"Alice makes potpourri-scented, dried flower petals for commercial accounts, Tess. Not flower arrangements." Tess sank into a chair as her mother told her this awful news.

Tyler, Tess's younger brother, hobbled into the room lugging a backpack in one hand and his horned toad's cage in the other. His leg was still shaky from last month's accident. "I say, old girl, what's all this talk about florists anyway?" the eight-year-old piped in. He faithfully practiced his British accent, which he studied every week on TV mystery shows, for his future career in Scotland Yard.

"It's just that Ms. M. and her fiancé had to give all the money they had saved to his niece. She's having a kidney transplant. So now they don't have money for flowers or a honeymoon, and Erin's a junior bridesmaid, and I'm not." Tess spoke in one long-winded gust. "I have to do something!"

"Whoa, Cupcake." Her father, Jim, stepped into the room from the back porch. "I could hear you all the way outside, even while cleaning the pool."

"Oh, hi, Dad. Maybe you can help." She gulped air and dove in again. "Do you know anyone who owns a florist shop?"

"Hmm." Mr. Thomas ran his hand through his thinning hair, which was the same coffee-colored shade as Tess's. Then he rubbed his whiskers. "No, I don't think I do. Sorry."

"Oh great." Tess sank into the kitchen chair again. "This was going to be my big chance to help. I can't do anything about the honeymoon or the flowers."

"What did you say about Erin's being a junior bridesmaid?" her mother asked, wiping her hands on a red-checked apron before hanging it over a wooden peg next to the sink.

"Oh, the niece who's having the operation was going to hand out flower petals for the guests to toss as Ms. M. and her new husband came out of the church. Now Erin's going to do it. Except it won't be flower petals. It's birdseed."

"Birdseed! I say, what a great plan," Tyler said.

"No! It hurts. Imagine getting pelted by birdseed. Now, unless you guys can help me, Ms. Martinez won't have any flowers at all. And for sure no honeymoon; although I can't do anything about that." Tess pulled herself out of her chair and went to the fridge. She popped the top of a Coke and let the bubbles sputter out some before drinking. She hated when it fizzed up her nose.

"Well, I just might have an idea," her dad said.

"Really?" Tess perked up. "What is it?"

"Last week in the Metro section of the paper I read that funeral homes are donating their used flowers after the services. How about if we call around to some funeral homes to see if we can use some after they've finished next Friday night? I'd even drive you over to pick them up."

Tess stared at her father. Could he be serious?

"Jim, are you kidding?" Her mother spoke first. "No woman in her right mind—desperate or not—wants used funeral flowers at her wedding."

Her father looked surprised. He was serious.

"Good show!" Tyler chimed in. "I say, I think it's a jolly good plan. And we could go to the cemeteries and gather all the wilted bouquets to collect enough petals to toss instead of that birdseed, what?"

"I think you're sick!" Tess said to her brother. She looked at her father. "I mean, thanks for the idea, Dad, but no thanks. I guess I'll just head to my room." She sighed. "And start my homework."

"Dinner's in an hour," her mother reminded her. Tess nodded, then walked down the long hallway and into her room. She flipped on her light switch, and her stereo came on at the same time as her lamp.

Now what? She started her computer and clicked on her diary program and began to type.

Dear Lord,

This is not good. I'm trying really hard not to be jealous that Erin gets to be a junior bridesmaid. It's because she's skinny, isn't it? And quieter in class. Now I can't help with the flowers or the honeymoon either. It's not just that I want to do something, Jesus; it's that I really want Ms. M.'s wedding to be nice. She's such a cool teacher, don't you think? And I deserve to help, too, right? I don't want to be left out.

A sharp knock on the door interrupted her thoughts, and she closed the screen quickly so no one could see.

"Who is it?" she called out.

"It's Mom."

"Come in." Tess swiveled in her chair to face her mother as she entered the room.

"Wooee, you had better clean this place up," her mother said, kicking aside a stack of dirty clothes growing on the floor.

"I know." Tess didn't feel like being reminded of that right now.

"I think I have an idea for Ms. Martinez," her mother offered.

"Really?" Tess sat up straight. "What?"

"Doesn't Janelle work at a flower shop? I'm sure she does. Last time I asked her if she could sit with Tyler, she said she would love to but she had a job at a flower shop on Shea Boulevard."

"Hey, I think you're right!" Tess exclaimed. Janelle used to be Tess's baby-sitter, and sometimes she still stayed with them when Tess's mother and father were out late. Janelle was also a Christian, the first person to mention Jesus to Tess. Last October Tess had become a Christian herself.

"Can I call her?" Tess asked.

"Go ahead," her mother said. "Then let me know what she says. Here's her number." She handed Tess a sticky note with a number scribbled on it.

"Thanks, Mom." Tess gave her mother a big hug before practically pushing her out the door. Her fingers flew across the keypad, punching in the numbers.

"May I speak with Janelle, please?' she asked.

"This is Janelle."

"Hi, this is Tess, you know, down the street?"

"Of course. How have you been?"

"Great, just great." Tess didn't want to chitchat right now. "What I'm wondering is, do you work at a florist shop?"

"Well…" Janelle's voice trailed off. Oh peachy, now she was going to be a dead end, too.

"I do, but not for long," Janelle finally said. "Why?"

Tess explained the situation as quickly as she could.

"I don't think they're going to give you anything, Tess. The owner is really mean. That's why I'm quitting. But I promised to stay a few more weeks until after the Mother's Day rush." Janelle paused, and Tess was just about to thank her anyway and hang up when Janelle spoke again.

"I could ask him for you, if you want. All he can do is say no, right?"

A tiny ember of hope glowed inside Tess's despairing heart. This was her only chance to help Ms. M. have a dreamy wedding. "Thanks, Janelle. And, Janelle, he does do pretty flowers, doesn't he?"

"They're awesome, even if he isn't," Janelle assured her. "I'll call you as soon as I know something." Then Janelle hung up.

five

Classy Gift

Friday, April 18

The next day Tess was eager to fill Erin in.

"So then what?" Erin leaned in close. Recess was almost over, and Tess rushed, wanting to cram it all in.

"Janelle couldn't believe it! She called back and said, if we help out tomorrow and Tuesday and Thursday after school next week, he would sell a small wedding package to Ms. M. for cost. He needs help to get ready for all the high-school proms next Friday. Janelle was amazed because he's usually so mean. But she said so many people have quit in the past couple of weeks that he was willing to take a chance."

Tess popped a Lemon Head into her mouth now that she was almost finished. "He's not paying us. We're working to earn the flowers. He'll sell them to Ms. M. for what it costs him. That way she has a really nice package for less than half-price. Cool, huh? And he's still getting a good deal. You will come with me and work, won't you?" Tess begged. "Please!"

"Of course. I'd better call my mom and ask her before recess is over." Erin stood up to walk to the pay phone in the hallway. She stopped and abruptly turned to face Tess.

"How are we going to get the rest of the money? You know, what it costs him?"

"Well," Tess walked back inside with her friend. "Janelle said it's about $250. I thought maybe we could go around at lunchtime and see if the class wanted to chip in. If everybody gave $10 as their wedding present, then she would have enough. It would be a great gift for her. Something we can all do." She remembered that Erin was doing something extra special and tried to dismiss her jealousy. It was a little easier now that she had something great to do, too.

"Isn't $10 a lot of money?" Erin asked.

"Yes," Tess answered. "But think about it, what else can you buy her for less? With wrapping paper, a card, and a bow, people would spend more. And if someone wants to give less, we'll just take whatever they give."

"You're right; great idea!" Erin pushed her sleeves up above her elbows. "Let's get to work!"

A few hours later, Tess ripped a piece of three-hole-punched paper from her science notebook and wrote on the top: *Sign up to donate $10 for Ms. Martinez's present of flowers for her wedding.*

"You should have unsnapped the notebook and not torn out the paper." Joann Waters sniffed as she looked at the jagged edge of the sign-up sheet. Tess turned to Erin and winked. Joann always wanted everything perfect.

"So are you going to sign up?" Tess asked. "I know you hate love and marriage and all that stuff."

"Yeah, I do." Joann said. "But I like Ms. M. so I'll sign up." She scribbled, "Joann, $10" on the paper. "I know I'd have to spend at least that much to buy something anyway, so why not?" She smiled. "Actually, I'm really looking forward to it. I wonder what her fiancé looks like?"

"Yeah, and her dress," Katie chimed in. "Do you think it will be long or short?"

"Definitely long," Tess said. "And I bet she has a beautiful veil, too."

"Well, we don't have long to wait!" Erin said. "Now, back to the flowers."

Paper in hand and pencils tucked behind their ears, the girls circulated around the lunchroom, explaining the situation to the rest of their classmates who chowed down greasy burritos and burpable hot dogs. The girls knew they would have an easy go with most people, but neither of them wanted to approach Kenny and Russell, the class cutups.

"Hi, girls, signing up people to be your friends this week?" Kenny joshed.

Tess could barely look at him. As he spoke, he stuffed a half-chewed hot dog into the pocket of his cheek, but little shreds of the meat escaped and splattered on the table in front of him.

Erin leaned close and whispered in Tess's ear, "There's nothing worse than feeding time at the zoo."

Tess giggled and continued, "No, we're signing up to collect money for Ms. M.'s wedding present. She couldn't buy any flowers, but if we each chip in ten dollars, she can get some. If you can't give that much, it's okay. We'll just chip in whatever we collect."

"I'll sign up," Russell said. Pleased, Tess handed him the sheet. Then he said, "But only if you order skunk weeds."

"Get out," Tess said. "What else were you going to buy her?"

Kenny and Russell looked at one another.

"Uh, I don't know," Kenny finally said.

"Come on, Kenny, let's sign up. My mom will be glad not to have to go to the store and find something. She's always complaining about how much wrapping paper costs." Russell scrawled his name across three lines.

Kenny printed his name underneath. "I hope the party after the wedding is cool. I hope they have some good chow."

Tess smiled. She knew the whole class—even Kenny— was eagerly anticipating Ms. M.'s wedding.

Erin spoke first as they walked away from the boys' table. "I guess that's everyone!"

Tess raised her hand, and Erin slapped her a high-five. Victory.

After lunch Tess told Ms. M. the good news, that Tess and Erin had found a florist who would give a 50 percent discount and that the class was contributing to the flowers. Ms. M.'s eyes filled with tears, and she asked Tess to take her seat.

"I am simply overwhelmed," Ms. Martinez said as she collected herself. "I want to tell you all how much I appreciate your gift. I truly appreciate your pitching in and cooperating. It's the best gift a teacher could ask for, to see that her students are thoughtful, considerate, and willing to work together. I'll order the flowers today after school." She smiled at Tess and slipped into her purse the scrap of paper on which Tess had written the florist's name.

Tess felt such a rush of love and purpose that she couldn't concentrate on her math lesson. She had done it; her plan was working! She doodled on her math book as she tried to plot another way to help Ms. M.

"What are you writing?" Erin whispered.

"Nothing," Tess said, quickly covering her sketch with her hand.

"Come on, the only secret we have is from everybody else—that we're sisters! We don't have secrets between us. Tell me!"

A wave of red the color of Hawaiian Punch washed over Tess's checks, but she moved her hand so Erin could see. Tess had written, *Tess E. Thomas* on her book. Tess's full name was Tess Elizabeth Thomas. But she had changed the *E* into an "and" sign by adding squiggles to the top and bottom of it. So now her message read *Tess & Thomas.*

Erin giggled. Thomas was Erin's big brother, Tom. Tess had a crush on him.

Tess quickly erased the names but smiled at her friend. Her secret was safe.

"Hey." Erin leaned across the aisle again. "I'm glad you said Janelle would be with us while we're at the florist's. I've never worked in a business before!" She smiled, then turned back to her math.

"Yeah." Tess smiled uneasily and turned back to her own book. Janelle hadn't said she was coming tomorrow morning. But she did work there. Tess recalled her parents had said Tess could only work at the florist's if Janelle was there. At the time, Tess had waved the restriction away in excitement.

But now…if Janelle didn't show up tomorrow, the whole plan was a bust.

six

Lies

Saturday Noon, April 19

Tess gave a sigh of relief as her mother jerked the car into a tight parking space in front of the flower shop. Janelle's little pink convertible was parked alongside the florist's van.

"Well, girls, we're here," Mrs. Thomas said. "Do you want me to come in with you?"

"No," Tess said. "Janelle is here; I'm sure she can take care of us."

"Right." Erin nodded her agreement.

"All right. I'll be back at 4:00. Don't work too hard!"

The girls clambered out of the Jeep and looked at one another, not moving, as Tess's mom raced out of the parking lot, almost toppling an ornamental shrub in the process.

Tess winced. "I hope no one was looking."

"I don't see anyone," Erin said. "I guess we had better go in, huh?"

Tess gulped. "Yeah, I guess so." The two of them gingerly pulled open the heavy door and walked into the shop. Bells jangled as the door shut behind them. A slap of cold air struck Tess across the cheek.

"May I help you find something?" A round man approached them, sweating in spite of the air conditioning.

"We're here to work. We're Janelle's friends." Tess offered her hand to shake his.

The man shook her hand coldly. His smile disappeared. "Well. You decided to show up. You're the two little urchins Janelle found. I guess I can find enough work for you to do since you practically begged to come in."

"Hi, girls." Janelle came out from one of the many walk-in coolers. "I just stopped in to say hello and to introduce you to Mr. Snodgrass. But I see you've already met."

Out of the corner of her eye, Tess watched Erin suppress a giggle. *Mr. Snodgrass!*

"Yes," Tess answered politely. "We've met."

"No more chattering. You're not here to socialize, you know. I plan to work you girls hard." Mr. Snodgrass turned to Janelle. "Would you show them the back room and set them up with prep stands and holders? If it's not too much to ask." He sniffed with contempt then went back to the front counter.

"Come on, you guys." Janelle opened a glass-paneled door into the back room.

Long rows of tables greeted them. Florist items were stacked or strung from every corner of the room. Ivy wire was gathered in bundles like stiff haystacks, and blocks of green floral foam lined the walls like cud-colored igloos.

"Look over there." Erin pointed. A long roll hung from the ceiling with yards and yards of ribbon attached to it. Some shone like silver bullets and some were soft blue, but all of them were beautifully spun. "What do you use those for?"

"We have a ribbon maker, see?" Janelle pointed to a wire hoop nearby. "We pull and wind the ribbon around to make bows for the floral decorations. It's really fun to match the ribbon to the flowers."

"I wonder which ones Ms. M. will choose," Tess whispered to Erin.

Janelle moved on toward the huge coolers in the back. "Here's where we store the flowers." She pulled open one of the massive doors. Even colder air rushed out—frigid, in fact. Shelves were stacked high with tiny, starlike baby's breath; thick-fingered lilies; paper-thin greenery; and shiny lemon leaves. Fluffy carnations looked like wrapped ribbons themselves.

"And in here," Janelle continued, "are the roses." Erin and Tess stepped into the next walk-in cooler.

"Oh, how beautiful," Erin breathed out. Tiny fists of flowers clung to the long-legged stems with shiny, triangular leaves. Jagged, razor-sharp thorns guarded the treasured blossoms.

"Why don't they smell good?" Tess asked.

"We keep them really cold so they stay fresh for a long time. When the warm air hits them, they start to open up, like this." She held her fist out in front of them, and then slowly uncurled her fingers, finally ending in a blossom-like cup.

"Oh. Will we get to work with the flowers?"

"I don't think so." Janelle shook her head. "We have a lot of flowers now because of several special orders and the prom. But Mr. Snodgrass is pretty picky about who does the flowers. Usually just the floral designers get to."

She tapped a large filing box. "Here's where we keep the orders. As soon as someone places an order, we put it in here based on its delivery date. See how thick it is for the prom next Friday?" Janelle fingered a thick file.

"I wonder if Ms. M.'s order is in there?" Tess said.

"Let's look." Janelle paged through the April 26 sheets. "Martinez? I don't see it. Maybe she hasn't come in to order yet."

"I thought she was coming yesterday," Erin said. Tess shrugged.

They walked away from the coolers and back into the room with all the tables.

"Today you'll be preassembling stuff." Janelle showed them how to set up the floral foam blocks in the many containers used for flower arrangements and how to cut the wires to anchor the projects that would be created later that day.

"So I guess you're set. Just clean up after yourselves and make sure you don't bother Mr. Snodgrass. I wouldn't even talk with him unless he talks to you first." Janelle took her sunglasses out of her purse and put them on. Then she pulled out her car keys.

"Are you leaving?" Tess asked her. A hard lump appeared in Tess's throat. A big lump.

"Yep. I don't work this Saturday. Got a date." Janelle smiled. "Don't worry; you'll do fine." She waved and walked out of the workroom door.

Tess sat on one of the folding chairs next to the table.

"You didn't know she was leaving?" Erin asked.

"No." Tess swallowed over and over again, but the lump wouldn't go away.

"It's okay. The work seems pretty easy," Erin assured Tess.

Yeah. That's not what I'm worried about. Mechanically, Tess reached for one of the cardboard arrangement boxes and placed a square of foam inside it. She looked around for the glue, but her mind wasn't on her work.

Erin's mom must not have told her she could only stay

when Janelle was there, or Erin would be a lot more upset. But Tess's mom had said that.

There was no turning back now. Ms. M.'s flowers were ordered, Tess hoped, and if the girls lost this job, they would have to tell her the flowers were off again. Tess imagined the tears flooding her teacher's eyes. Or worse, Tess would have to ask her parents for the extra $250 to pay for the flowers.

God, I know you understand that I have to stay no matter what my parents said. This is the only way to get the flowers for Ms. M. If I don't get her the flowers, I'll really let her down. Not to mention having nothing great to do for her wedding.

Her prayer was interrupted by Mr. Snodgrass as he walked into the workroom. "I see you're working." He coolly surveyed their activities. Erin's box was put together well, but Tess's was a mess. How could she keep her mind on her work?

"This isn't right." He pointed at her box. "Ask your friend." He jerked his thumb at Erin. "She will show you how to assemble an acceptable unit."

Embarrassment flooded Tess, and she felt tears pushing up under her eyelids.

He turned to leave, but then he abruptly turned back. "You do have experience with flowers and arrangements, don't you?" He pointed at Tess.

How could he expect me to have experience; I'm only twelve! But maybe Janelle thought Tess did and had said so. If she told him no, she would have to call her mom to come and pick her up. And this whole deal would be over. No flowers for Ms. M.; humiliation for Tess.

Then she remembered she had helped to trim azalea bushes last year. They were flowers, right? "Yes," she answered.

"Fine." Mr. Snodgrass left the workroom.

Erin looked questioningly at Tess but didn't say anything. She did have experience. But in her heart, she knew that's not the kind he was talking about. The lie wrapped around her heart and squeezed like a python. Her breath raced and came out in little pants.

What else could she do? She was trapped. All she could think of was to keep working and hope nobody found out the truth.

seven

Caught

Saturday Evening, April 19

By the time Tess finished work for the day, she was exhausted. But she still had a long hike ahead of her with her dad. The drive to one of their hiking mountains was painfully quiet.

"Did you have a good day?" Tess asked her father, hoping to start a conversation.

"Not really," he answered. Then he didn't say anything else.

Tess picked at the laces on her hiking boots. The red strings were wearing through; she would have to buy a new pair before they hiked the Rim-to-Rim next month. Flexing her calf muscles, she thought about that hike. When her dad had first asked her, she thought she couldn't complete the difficult hike. But now, after months of training, she was sure she could.

"We're here," her father said, his voice clipped. He hopped out of the car and adjusted his water bottle and baseball cap. He set off toward the top of the hill without even looking at Tess.

A nervous sweat sprinkled her skin, and it wasn't from the

warm desert evening. She caught a look at his face. It was as smooth and emotionless as the rocks that formed the cliffs towering over the paths to either side. Normally, Tess would have admired the punchy little brittle weeds that grew from the crevices all around her. Today, although they turned their yellow faces toward her, she walked right by.

Soon they reached the mountaintop, which, strangely, was almost abandoned tonight. A light wind blew around them, causing an eerie, wheezing noise as it rounded the corners. Tess's dad sat down, and she sat beside him. But not too close.

He uncapped his water bottle, took a swig, and set it down. "Was Janelle with you all day today?" he asked.

Bull's-eye. She was dead.

"Um, why?" Tess asked, knowing it was useless to try to buy time but did it by instinct anyway.

"I was doing errands today, and I saw her little pink car on the road. At first I thought it was someone else, but then a few hours later—an hour before you came home—I saw her drive down our street and park in her driveway."

Tess gulped. The big, hard lump was back.

She stared at a desert paintbrush plant, not knowing what to say. Her face felt as red as the tips of the plant. Oh, to dry up and blow away like its feathery fronds.

"Janelle didn't stay the whole time." Tess gulped again, fear closing her throat as she talked with a cotton-dry tongue. "She left after she showed us what to do."

Her father sat stone still. He finally looked at her, and she saw the anger beneath his calm look. "And did your mother tell you that you could stay only as long as Janelle was there?"

"Yes."

"So by staying the entire time and not calling us or telling us that she had left, you decided on your own that it was better to lie."

"Well, I didn't think about it that way." The sweat trickled down her spine now. "Mr. Snodgrass, the owner, said that Ms. M. had ordered her flowers, and I was afraid that if I called, you would make me leave. Then Ms. M. wouldn't have any flowers. And I'd hurt her. And look dumb." Was that another lie? Did Mr. Snodgrass say the flowers had been ordered? Tess couldn't remember.

"Don't you think you look pretty dumb getting caught in a lie?" Her father shook his head. "I just don't know what's going on with you. Maybe you need some closer supervision. Maybe I've had enough of your going to church and doing things with people I know nothing about." He yanked his laces and tightened them before heading back down the hill.

"It's not that, Dad. I just didn't know what to do. I'm not even really sure he said she had ordered, come to think of it."

"Did you know lying was wrong?"

What could she say? "Yes. It's just that I thought I'd lose the flowers. And it was my plan. I needed to make sure it came out okay."

He kept walking. "Would you have told me about this if I hadn't caught you?" The setting sun cast a long, scary shadow of him against a crooked boulder.

Tess didn't answer for a minute. "I don't know. It doesn't feel good to lie. But I want that stuff for Ms. M. She can't have a honeymoon, and at least I wanted her to have the flowers. So I was going to do it anyway, I guess."

He looked at her. "Well, that's one honest thing you've said today. No more lies. Do you understand?"

"Yes," Tess said.

"And there will be consequences for this. I'm not sure what they'll be yet; I need to talk with your mother." He marched down the hill, and Tess worked hard to keep up.

"But I'll tell you one thing," he said, walking by a sprouting orange sneezeweed. "There had better not be any more lies."

"I know," Tess said. The python around her heart squeezed again as she remembered she had told Mr. Snodgrass she had experience working with flowers. And Tess couldn't help but worry what punishment her parents would decide on for the lie she had been caught in.

Late that night, after the house was still and even the streetlights flickered, Tess tossed in her bed. Finally getting up, she turned on her computer and clicked onto her prayer diary.

Lord, if you had made Ms. M. choose me for the bridesmaid, none of this would have happened. I wouldn't have had to do all these crazy things to help with the wedding. I wanted to do something for her, too. Then I tried my best to make things work out okay. And look what's happened!

As soon as the words were written, she felt sorrow like a heavy brick.

I'm sorry, Jesus, for blaming you. I know it was my own fault I lied. I'm sorry, and now it's over. I didn't really lie to Mr. Snodgrass, right? Just stretched the truth a little. Please help me to tell the truth from now on.

She shut down the computer and slipped between the sheets again, not feeling any better than before she had prayed.

eight

Tyler's Two Surprises

Sunday Morning, April 20

Sunday morning was a rush for Tess, as always. "I guess I'll call Erin to see if she remembers whether I'm supposed to bring my testimony," Tess mumbled, looking for the phone. The Spring Fling was next month, and the youth pastor had asked Tess—Tess!—to tell everyone how she had received Jesus. A mix of happiness and worry mingled in her mind as she searched through her drawers for the piece of paper she had written her testimony on. Now, where was the phone?

"Aha." Pulling a damp towel off her dresser, she found the phone. She picked up the receiver and prepared to dial, when, Wham! It hit her. What was that gross smell? Like, like, rotten fish.

Could it be the towel? She sniffed it. A little musty but no fish. She looked at the phone again. Pee-yew! She sniffed the handle. Gross. She unscrewed the cap on the part she spoke into.

"Tyler!" she screamed, racing down the hall. "Did you let Big Al into my room?" Her stocking feet skidded to a stop in front of Tyler's room.

"I say, was it quite a frightful surprise?" He giggled. Big Al was Tyler's disgusting best friend and Tess's number-one enemy.

"I can't believe you let him put a piece of canned fish in my phone. Pick it out and spray some Lysol on it. Now!" Disgusting. The rotten fish smell would be in her nose all day.

"I say, old girl, let's not raise the blood pressure. I thought it was a brilliant example of practical jokery."

"Tyler, you know I'm in a hurry on…"

Tess was about continue when she noticed he was already dressed. Neatly. And on a Sunday morning.

"What are you doing up so early? Hercules got the flu?"

Tyler was famously attached to his pet horned toad, Hercules.

"Fancy that. Surprise number two," he said. Tess saw he was serious now. "I, uh, thought maybe I'd go to church with you this morning. If that's all right with you."

The phone receiver slipped from her fingers and clattered to the floor. "All right? You have to be kidding. That's great!" She hugged her brother. *Thank you, Lord!* she shouted inside. After picking up the phone and tossing it onto his bed, she asked, "Did you talk to Mom and Dad about this?"

"Nooo…" Tyler coughed. "I thought you might help me out there, old bean." His big, leaf-green eyes looked up. Pity washed over her. Knowing her dad's dislike of Christianity, this wasn't going to be easy. *But then*, she thought, as she grabbed her brother's hand, *nothing worthwhile is ever easy. And what's more worthwhile than this?*

"All right," she said. "But I'm not kidding about your cleaning up my phone. Today." Tyler giggled, and Tess tried hard not to laugh herself.

They walked down the hallway and into the bright,

lemon-fresh kitchen. Sunlight raced in through the open windows and danced around the walls, twirling through the curtains as it came.

"Hi, Mom. Hi, Dad." Tess used her happiest voice. She hoped her parents weren't still angry about yesterday's lie.

"Hi. Tyler, why are you dressed so early? What a surprise!" Their father smiled, then folded his newspaper section in half and set it down. He picked up his coffee and sipped.

"I, um, thought I might go to church with Tess today."

Tess looked at Tyler, he looked at the floor. *Poor guy. He's so nervous he forgot to use his accent.*

"Church? Tess, did you invite him again?"

"No, Dad, I asked her myself." Tyler looked up now. "I want to go. I had fun last time, and I've been thinking about it a lot. I…I even prayed."

Tess could barely keep the smile from her lips.

"I don't know. Things are changing around here, and I feel as if I have nothing to say about it." Mr. Thomas stacked the newspapers, not looking at them while he did. Tess's mother moved behind him and put her hand on his shoulder while resting the other hand on her large tummy.

"I don't think it would do any harm, Jim," she said. "Overall, I've seen some great changes in Tess since she's been going to that church." She looked at Tess and smiled. Tess knew her mom was thinking about the lie yesterday, but Tess was glad her mom didn't bring it up now. "And I always did want the kids to have some spiritual education."

"Great. Now my own wife is against me. What next? If we had a dog, he would probably take sides, too."

Tess dared to smile when she heard that. Victory! Dad was still lathered up about the idea of Tyler going to church, but if he was telling jokes, she knew they had won.

"It'll be okay, Dad. I promise I'll look out for him."

"Yes, I know you will." He picked up his paper again and looked at Tyler. "Go ahead. This time anyway."

"Thanks, Dad." Tyler kissed his mom, then patted her tummy. "'Bye, baby!" he sang out before running to the hallway to put on his shoes.

Tess stood closer to her father. "Thanks from me, too, Dad."

"Yep, Muffin, it's all right. But," he pulled down the paper to look at her, "we haven't finished talking about yesterday. It just may be that you won't go to the wedding. Or work at the flower shop again."

Tess's heart jumped. But then he dropped the really big bomb. "Or maybe no more church. Maybe we need to spend more time together as a family on Sundays. Then we would have time to talk about these things."

Tess nodded. She didn't say anything. She knew if she did, her dad might explode and ruin the day for Tyler. She practically tiptoed across the cool kitchen tile and into the carpeted hall. She checked her watch. Too late to call Erin now. She would be on her way to pick up Tess. After fishing a pair of shoes out of the hall closet, she looked up at her brother.

Tyler was peeking out the door's window, watching for Erin's family. Tess felt joy pour through her again, washing away her fear and anxiety. Tyler said he had prayed. Maybe he was closer than she thought.

nine

The Message

Sunday Morning, April 20

"I'm so excited your brother could come!" Erin squeezed Tess's hand on the way to their classroom. Erin's younger brother, Josh, had taken Tyler to the third-grade boys' classroom.

"I know. He looked, um, much happier than the last time we came," Tess said. "But," a grim look passed across her face, "I know someone who wasn't too happy."

They entered the doorway to the sixth-grade Sunday school classroom. As usual, their teachers, Sjana and Adam, were setting up props. A long table sat in front of a white dry-erase board. A CD player and speakers sat on the table, but they apparently didn't plan to use the CD player today. Tess spotted Adam's guitar up front.

Tess loved the class. Her teachers, high-schoolers, always had awesome lessons. The singing was the best though.

"Was it your dad?" Erin asked as they found seats near the back. "Was he mad?"

"Yep." Tess sat down on the gray-green upholstered chair. "He said the whole family was against him and maybe I'd better stop going to church so we could spend more time together as a family on Sunday." She slipped her feet out of her shoes and stood in her stocking feet.

Slivers of ice pierced her heart. She wasn't telling Erin the whole truth. She hadn't come clean about the lies, which were what really made her dad mad. Sisters never kept secrets from each other, like Erin said the other day. Until now.

Tell her, a voice whispered in Tess's heart.

I *can't*, she whispered back. The cold slivers dug in even deeper.

"Well," Erin continued, "even if you can't come to church, there's nothing that can take Jesus away from you now. You're his, and he'll live inside your heart forever."

Yeah, Tess thought, *but how does he feel about living with lies?*

"I'm going to get a drink," Erin said. "And some donuts. You want any?"

"No," Tess answered. "I'm not hungry."

A minute later Adam rapped his knuckles on the table in front of him. "Hey there, settle down. Let's start with a little praise music." He strummed a few strings on his guitar. Adam started to sing just as Erin sidled up alongside Tess.

"Hey, Frosty," Tess teased her, brushing the powdered sugar off Erin's chin and shoulder. Erin had already demolished the donut.

Then Tess sang in a clear, strong voice, "I love you, Lord, and I desire to seek after you every day. Let me walk in your way, I pray."

In spite of herself, Tess smiled. Praise did that to her. *Please, God, let Tyler have a good time in his class, and let him come back to church, and me, too. Help someone to explain Jesus' gift to him. I will, if you want.*

"We're sitting down now." Erin tugged on Tess's arm.

"We'll sing a little more in a bit," Adam said. "But first, we have a great lesson." He opened a plastic container then walked around and handed each person a square of dark brown chocolate.

"Hey, a new snack. Can I have another one?" Robert, the kid in front of Tess, called out. If Tess didn't know better, she would think he was Big Al's brother. Obnoxious.

"Only if you promise to eat it." Adam handed him another piece, but Tess noticed a sparkle in Adam's eye.

"No problem, man." Robert snagged the chocolate and took a bite.

"Blech!" He practically spat it out. Everyone else was biting into the chocolate, too.

"Gross. It tastes like dirty wax," Erin said.

Tess wished she had a Kleenex. She would spit the candy out.

"So what's the matter, guys?" Adam said. "Don't like the candy?"

"No!" everyone shouted back.

"That's because it's unsweetened. It has no sugar in it."

"It's bitter," someone said.

"Exactly." Adam wrapped up the leftovers and set them on the table at the front of the room. "Very bitter. And it leaves a bad taste in your mouth. Now," he started walking the aisles again, this time unwrapping several Hershey's chocolate bars as he talked.

"Anybody want to try one of these?" He waved the chocolate above his head.

"Sure." Robert was the first to answer.

"Really? After that nasty experience?"

"Yeah. That one might be the real thing." Adam smiled and handed one to Robert.

"Don't eat it until everyone else has a piece," Adam said. After he handed them all out, Tess took a bite. This time the chocolate was creamy and sweet. Not at all like the other bar.

"Anyone in here ever have a bad burger?" Sjana asked.

"Yes, ugh," several students called back.

"Did you eat another burger after that?"

"Of course," people murmured.

"Well," Adam said, as he headed to the front of the room, "that's how some people feel about church. They tried it once or maybe twice. They had a bad experience. Maybe people didn't talk to them or were rude, or the visitors didn't like the singing. Whatever. It left a bitter taste."

Adam held up a piece of the dark chocolate. Robert plugged his nose.

"But we have to reach out to them still. Tell them that the next one might be sweet. Like Christ. Like this one." Adam held up the Hershey's bar. "God says to us in the Bible, 'Taste and see that I am good.' So,"—he motioned to Sjana to start handing out papers—"when you invite people to the Spring Fling, which is in thirteen days, you'll know what to say if they tell you they've tried church and didn't like it. Our theme is, 'New Life,' like when new plants come forth in spring and new baby animals are born, you know. It's a chance for your friends to have new life, too."

"Yeah, we'll ask them if they ever had a bad burger," someone called out.

"And if they ever ate burgers again," Robert said.

"Right," Adam said. "And you can tell them about our great speaker, Tess Thomas!"

"Yeah! Go Tess, go Tess!" People whistled and waved to her.

Red crept up Tess's neck, but she was happy to be a part of the class. And ready to share her faith. She snagged two of the invitations as they were passed around. On one she wrote "Joann" and on the other one "Katie." She flashed them at Erin, who nodded her approval. Then Tess tucked them into her Bible. She wanted to do for Katie and Joann what her Secret Sister had done for her: introduce them to Jesus. She would give them the invitations this week. Fun! Ms. M.'s wedding next weekend, Spring Fling the weekend after.

Oh, yeah, Ms. M.'s wedding. And flowers. And a lie to Mr. Snodgrass. The slivers in her heart drove in deeper. All she had meant to do was plan a way to give her teacher something good. How had it gone so wrong?

"All right," Sjana said. "Open your Bibles."

Tess opened her Bible but didn't flip to the section Sjana talked about. Instead, she unfolded the Spring Fling brochure and started to read it. She couldn't believe she was the speaker. Awesome.

A verse, Colossians 3:10, was listed as the Spring Fling's theme. Instead of listening to Sjana's lesson, Tess wanted to read the verse right away. After all, she was part of the program. She licked her fingers and silently flicked through the pages looking for Colossians. Where was it? Please don't call on me. She had no idea what Sjana was talking about.

After about fifty years she found Colossians 3:10. "You have begun to live the new life. In your new life you are being made new. You are becoming like the One who made you. This new life brings you the true knowledge of God." Amazing. It was just how she felt, too. New.

She lifted her eyes to read the verses that came before it, like Adam had taught them last month. Fear froze her. "Do not lie to each other. You have left your own sinful life and the things you did before." She sat, chewing her pencil eraser. She had left her old life, hadn't she? If she had, she had no choice.

"Okay, make sure you answer those questions this week," Sjana said, snapping shut her Bible. What questions? Tess had missed the lesson. She would have to ask Erin later.

"Let's sing," Adam said, strumming his callused fingertips against the silky, strong guitar strings. "I have another song for you, an old one. I'll put the words on the overhead so we can read them through a few times."

Tess read the words, "I have decided, I'm going to do what I say I believe, no more room in me to deceive." A hidden ball of strength grew inside her. Tess had a new life. She was going to tell the truth, no matter what. And she was going to start by confessing her lie to Mr. Snodgrass.

Visions of his kicking her out of the store, of Ms. M. standing at the altar with no flowers passed through Tess's mind. But the icicles in her heart thawed a little, and she knew she was on the right track. She was going to tell Mr. Snodgrass she had no floral experience at all. No matter what awful thing he did to her. And she was certain it would be awful.

ten

The Countdown

Monday, April 21

"So what do you think?" Erin showed Tess her geography report.

"Nice," Tess answered, looking through the folder. A world map was the first page, with Canada outlined in bold black. Then Victoria was highlighted in red. Erin had used Tess's computer last week to type the report.

"I hope it's enough extra credit," Erin said.

"I'm sure it will be. Come on," Tess whispered so nobody, especially Kenny and Russell, could hear her. "I have a lot to tell you."

The two sneaked into the reading corner.

Erin bent her head close to Tess's. "So what did your dad say last night?"

"Nothing. I am so nervous! He wasn't home when we got back from church. He had business clients in from out of town, and he spent the whole day and evening with them." Tess fumbled a Lemon Head out of her pocket and popped it into her mouth. She swirled it around the inside of her cheek until her mouth puckered from the sour. "I hope his business went well, or he'll be doubly mad."

She cracked the Lemon Head between her jaws and continued, "But he told my mom to tell me we're hiking tonight. Which is weird because it's Monday. We never hike on Monday. I guess they decided on something, and he'll tell me tonight."

"Scary." Erin leaned back into the corner. "I never want to be alone with my parents when I know I'm in trouble. Especially with my dad. It's better to have other people around. Being alone in trouble reminds me of a story my grandma told me. In the old days my grandpa took the dogs that went bad far into the mountains. Then he came back alone." She folded a stick of Doublemint into her mouth. She grinned at Tess. They always chewed Doublemint, since they were the double sisters.

"I don't think he's going to shoot me," Tess said.

"I didn't mean he was," Erin said quickly. "I just meant, well, I don't like to hear bad news alone."

"I know." Tess slumped down even farther. "Especially from Dad."

"Well, I'm proud of the way you're dealing with it," Erin added with a cheerful smile.

Tess leaned back into the bookshelf. The reading area wasn't too cozy, just a large corner made by joining two bookshelves and then throwing down an old carpet scrap. It smelled moldy, as if the carpet had been left out in the rain and hadn't dried all the way. But that wasn't the only reason Tess was uncomfortable.

"Erin, don't be proud of me. I have to tell you something," Tess said. She chewed the center of another Lemon Head and picked a sticky piece from her molar before continuing.

"Yeah?"

"Promise you'll still be my best friend?"

"Of course."

"Well, the real reason my dad is so steamed is because I lied to him." Tess spat out the words. Her heart lightened, but the bitter flavor of the lie still stung her tongue on the way out.

"You did?" Erin's eyes grew large. "About what?"

"Well, when we were at the flower shop last Saturday, I was supposed to stay only as long as Janelle was there. So when she left, I should have called home. But I didn't. I stayed because I was worried Mr. Snodgrass wouldn't give Ms. M. the flowers and stuff. But then I didn't tell my parents either. So I was lying, you know, by letting them think Janelle stayed."

"Oh, wow." Erin unraveled a piece of the carpet fibers, which were coiled into tough little rings. She peeled one away from the ragged rubber edge on the floor. "No wonder you asked if my parents cared. My parents freak if I ever lie, even a little."

"Yeah, I know." Tess's head felt light and dizzy with worry. "Mine did. And I'm sorry I wasn't honest with you either. I didn't really lie, but I didn't tell you my parents said I couldn't stay. I'm sorry. I was mad at you because Ms. M. picked you to be the junior bridesmaid."

"Are you still mad?"

"No. Sometimes I'm still a little jealous, but I'm trying not to be."

Erin gave her sister a quick shoulder hug then moved back and looked into her eyes.

"That's not all." Tess unfolded her crossed legs and overlapped them the opposite way.

"Uh-oh. I don't like the tone of your voice." Erin scooted closer.

"Remember when I told Mr. Snodgrass I had experience?" Tess leaned toward Erin's ear, not wanting Ms. M. to overhear.

"Yeah…"

"Well, I think he meant had I worked with flowers in a store or craft fair or had someone teach me or something. But I, uh, just worked in my yard. But I had to say yes!" Tess defended. "He was like, freaking out, and I was afraid he would send me home. I didn't expect him to be such a madman."

"I understand," Erin said. "But maybe that's not what he meant. Maybe he meant, if you hadn't had experience, he would have Janelle show you since your box was sort of messy when he stepped in. He didn't ask me if I had experience. And I don't."

"Oh, I guess he could have meant that." Tess interlaced her fingers. Maybe all of this would have worked out anyway, without her lying. She doubted it. Her parents definitely would have made her go home. "But anyway, I knew it was a lie. And yesterday the Lord showed me that I am new and shouldn't be lying."

"Cool!" Erin said. "So now what are you going to do?"

"What choice do I have?" Tess said. "I have to tell Mr. Snodgrass."

Just then someone slipped some books into the shelf right behind them. It was Ms. M.

"Hi, girls," she said, her black hair clipped back into a silver lizard clasp. She bent down to their level. "Thank you again for the flowers. What a lovely, lovely idea. I had been thinking how silly I was to tell you my problems, and then when you worked out such a thoughtful solution, I thought, You know, maybe there was a purpose in my telling the girls that after all."

She smiled and stood up again. "I ordered the flowers last Friday, and they'll deliver them to the church Saturday. There's nothing to be done about the honeymoon, but at least I'll have beautiful flowers for my wedding. I chose lavender roses, which mean 'our love will be happy.' And Erin," she said, "don't forget about the dress fitting Thursday night."

"I won't," Erin promised.

Ms. M. walked away.

"I can't wait to see her in her dress," Tess said. "And the church all done up. I wonder if Kenny and Russell will wear suits? Do you think she ordered a bouquet to toss besides the one she's keeping?"

"I don't know," Erin said. "Depends on how much she could get in that small package." The two of them stood up and stretched, now that free time was over.

"I'm surprised she ordered her flowers last Friday. We didn't see her name in the order file," Tess said.

"That's right!" Erin said. "Maybe Mr. Snodgrass was waiting to see how we worked out before he ordered the flowers."

"Oh." Tess hoped that he had ordered them already and wasn't waiting until Tuesday, when he might toss her out of the shop.

Erin squeezed Tess's hand. "Well, I'll be praying for you. Now that you have to tell your dad about the second lie, you'll really need it." She rambled back to her desk.

Tess's face froze. Tell her dad? Oh no, this kept getting worse and worse. She hadn't thought about that. But, if she was going to be honest, she had to tell him. This "thoughtful solution" had turned into a mess.

The big, hard lump in her throat was back to stay. Telling the truth after telling a lie was a hundred times harder than she thought.

eleven

Truth and Consequences

Monday Evening, April 21

Tess jumped out of the car as if she were leaping off a hot griddle. Her dad had said nothing about her discipline all the way to the hiking trail. He had talked about other things and seemed happy. Well, not exactly happy.

"Isn't that the Janssen's Suburban over there?" he asked, as he adjusted his baseball cap.

"Yes," Tess said. That must mean Tom was here. He and his dad hiked, too. She ran back to the car and peeked at her reflection in the car's mirror while her dad wasn't looking. Not great, but okay. She tucked in her shirt. How much anxiety could she take in one night?

"Ready?" her dad asked. Tess thought he sounded a little impatient.

"Ready," she answered.

The two of them began the long climb. The mountain wasn't as flat as the one they had hiked last week. This trail curved around lots of crumbling, graham-cracker-colored boulders. Small gravel tumbled out of the nooks and crannies like crushed cookies. Spiny, peeling yuccas camped along the side of the path, and dried pieces of old cacti littered the mountainside. Tess huffed. This trail was as steep as attic stairs.

"Getting too difficult?" her dad called back over his shoulder.

"No," Tess gasped out. They turned a corner and saw Mr. Janssen and Tom, who were on their way down.

"Hi there," Mr. Janssen called out, waving. Within a minute or two they met at a bend in the path.

"We seem to meet a lot these days," Tess's dad said, smiling for the first time that night.

"That we do, that we do," Erin's dad said. He moved over to talk with Tess's dad while Tom moved closer to Tess and out of earshot of their fathers.

"Hi, Tess," he said. "How's it going?"

"Okay," she said, hoping he couldn't tell how breathless she felt.

"Getting ready for the Rim-to-Rim next month?" he asked.

"Yeah, I'm ready." Tess smiled.

"Hmm." Tom ran his fingers through his hair that was the same butterscotch color as Erin's. "My sister told me your dad might ground you from going to church."

Tess bit a hangnail. Surely her Secret Sister kept the secret about the lie.

"Well, I think it's pretty brave to keep talking to him about church," Tom said. "I prayed for you today."

"You did?" Her mouth dropped. Back to gasping for air again.

"Yeah. So have a good hike," he said. Then he strolled back to where his dad was standing.

"We had better get going, huh, Tom?" Mr. Janssen said.

"Yeah," Tom answered. "Good seeing you." He waved to Tess and her dad.

Tess's father walked behind her as they started out again and the trail grew even more abrupt.

"I'm okay, Dad. I'm not going to trip again," she said. In January she had tripped and twisted her ankle. Now her dad always wanted to walk behind her on the steep parts.

"I know." But he still stayed behind her. Saying nothing. All his chatty talk had stopped as soon as the Janssens had left.

Dusk was dropping slowly. Saguaro cacti blossoms cracked open, like they did each evening, so the desert bats could pollinate them. But her mind wasn't really on the trail. Bats seemed just about the right mood for her. She and her father must have passed twenty or thirty hikers on the trail, but Tess wasn't counting. She was lost in her thoughts.

"We're here," her dad announced as they climbed to the top of the trail. They sat down on a smooth, flat stone that made a perfect natural bench.

Tess caught her breath and took a swig of water. So did her dad. Minutes slipped by before he started to talk. His voice was barbed. He rubbed his temples with one hand.

"You knew your mother and I trusted you, and you broke that trust. It never crossed my mind that you would disobey me like that and then lie about it. I'm very disappointed."

Tess's head hung low, like a broken flower on a slim stem.

"I'm glad I went out for business last night. I was so upset I didn't want to speak with you. Do you realize you could have been hurt or kidnapped or worse at that place? We have no idea who that man is!"

He swigged his water and gulped it down. "If you just would have called us and told us the truth, we could have helped. Maybe Mom would have come to the shop and stayed while the two of you worked."

Oh. She hadn't thought of that. Maybe it wasn't always up to her alone to figure things out.

Her dad continued, "Today I spent some time thinking of the consequences you should pay for lying. I figured that I'd forbid you to go to Ms. Martinez's wedding."

"Dad!" Tess wailed. "The whole class is looking forward to it. Please let me go!"

The sun melted a little lower into the mountain as her father continued. "But your mother said—correctly—that would punish Ms. Martinez, too. Then I thought perhaps you should just not go back to the florist shop."

Tess considered it. She would never have to see Mr. Snodgrass again. Then her smile flipped upside down. Ms. M. would have no flowers. A bare wedding. Not only no tossing bouquet but not even one to keep. On top of the ruined plans for a honeymoon, it would be a sad day for Ms. M. And it all would be Tess's fault.

"What we settled on is to ground you for two weeks, not including the wedding or the flower shop. But no going anywhere else for two weeks, and no phone calls for a week. It's going to take awhile before you earn back our full trust." He stood up. "Do you understand?"

"Yes, Dad." Tess nodded solemnly. That didn't seem too bad when she considered what it might have been.

"But wait!" she suddenly blurted out. "What about Spring Fling at church? That's in twelve days; I'm supposed to be the speaker."

"Sorry, Tess. No go." Her dad swigged his water and sat back on the rock.

"Why do you hate church so much?" Tess blurted out, not thinking.

Her father's face hardened. "You're grounded because you lied, miss, not because I hate church."

"Um, yeah, I know." Tess forced herself to take a deep

breath. "I'm sorry. But you do hate church, don't you?"

Her dad sat quietly for a minute, waiting for some hikers to go down the hill. "I don't hate church, Tess. But I don't like church either. I visited a church with a friend when I was in high school. I thought maybe I'd be interested in God. I'd been praying a little. Well, anyway, when I visited the church, the people ignored me. They played Bible games I didn't understand. I remember one time I guessed Barnabas was an apostle, and they all laughed."

Tess sat as still as the chain-fruit cholla bushes next to her. Poor dad. He must have felt really bad.

"The adults weren't much better. That same friend and I used to hang out together. When his family found out I didn't go to that church, they wouldn't let him come over anymore. I just decided," he said, "that I don't need that kind of deal. I didn't want my kids to have the same experience."

Anger, sadness, fear, and protectiveness pumped through Tess's heart. She couldn't keep track of them all. The words came to her mouth before they passed through her brain almost. "Have you ever had a bad hamburger?"

"What?" Her dad looked at her like she had had too much sun. Only it was evening.

"Did you ever eat a bad hamburger?" she persisted.

"Yes." His forehead wrinkled with curiosity. "Why?"

"Did you eat another one later, or did you never eat a burger again?"

"Of course I ate other ones. What are you getting at?"

"Well," Tess said, "church can be like that. Just because one is bad doesn't mean the others are. You could try another one. Mine isn't like that." She had said it. She had meant to tell that to Joann and Katie and had no idea the burger example was for her dad.

"You have me there, kiddo." He smiled and ruffled her hair. Tess relaxed a bit and scooted just a centimeter closer to her dad. He still loved her. "But even if your church is a good one, I really don't need church."

"Not church, Dad. Jesus."

Her father frowned.

"Can I tell you something, Dad?" Tess gulped the lump down.

"Sure."

"Please let me tell the whole thing," she said. Prickles ran up her spine. "There's another lie I didn't tell you about."

Her dad looked as though he was about to say something.

"Let me finish, okay, Dad?" she asked in her most respectful voice.

He nodded.

"I was thinking, okay, I got busted for lying. But I knew I had told another lie. I was hoping I wouldn't get caught again. But yesterday at church I felt the Lord leading me to a part of the Bible that says I am new now that I am a Christian, and this new person doesn't lie. After that, I felt sure of what I had to do. The other day I told Mr. Snodgrass I had experience working with flowers, when I don't. I said that because I was scared. But I'm going to apologize and tell him the truth tomorrow. Even if he tells me Ms. M.'s flower order is off." Tess waited for her dad to say something.

"He just might say that, Tess. But I appreciate your new-found honesty." He still didn't look happy. But then she couldn't expect him to either.

A lonely whippoorwill called in the creeping dark. Tess continued, "On my own, I felt bad about lying. But I wasn't honest until I was caught. But when I was in church, I was sure I should do something about the lie I didn't get caught in. I needed to tell the truth no matter what the consequences."

"I believe you, Muffin. And because you told me before you were caught, I won't add to your discipline. But you're still going to have to cancel speaking at the Spring Fling. Even if your church serves good burgers." He smiled and stopped rubbing his forehead.

Then he frowned again. "Maybe I should go with you when you talk to the florist. From what you girls say, this Mr. Snodgrass just might fly off the handle."

"Maybe," Tess answered. "Or maybe Mom could sit in the car outside the shop in case he boots me out."

"Whatever you decide, you may not stay there one second without Janelle or another adult. Do you understand?" Her father looked stern, but she caught the smile underneath.

"I understand." She wished she didn't have to go back for one second even when Janelle was there. But Tess couldn't back out; Ms. M. said she already had placed her order.

But no Spring Fling. No giving her testimony for the very first time, no sharing her new life with Katie and Joann. Her heart felt thick with sadness. And she would have to tell Pastor Jack. How embarrassing! What if he couldn't find someone else?

twelve

Money Collectors

Tuesday at Lunch, April 22

"Okay, let's collect the money." The Sisters gobbled their food and ran from table to table in the lunchroom, collecting ones and fives and tens from everyone in Ms. M.'s class. Some bills were folded into wads, mostly so no one could see how much or how little someone was giving. Some were almost gray from the hundreds of hands they had passed through. Some were ripped or wrinkled. But it didn't matter. They needed to give Mr. Snodgrass the money tonight.

"Here's my cash." Kenny handed over a ten. "Don't forget, stinkweed."

Tess rolled her eyes before stuffing his money into the brown envelope she had brought from home. Then she smiled. She knew Kenny couldn't wait for the wedding—and the reception party afterward. Now that Ms. M. and her new husband had no honeymoon trip planned, they could stay at the reception as long as they wanted. Good thing they had paid for the musicians and the cake before they gave away the rest of their wedding savings.

After the girls had collected the money, they sat down at a lunch table.

"Did you bring the Spring Fling invitations?" Erin asked.

"Yeah. But I'm sort of embarrassed to tell Joann and Katie that I can't go. I mean, I invited them and everything."

"I'm still going." Erin said.

Yeah right, Tess thought. *Without me.*

"I guess I'd better call Pastor Jack after school and tell him he needs to find someone else to speak," Tess said. "I crumpled up my testimony last night and threw it away." She put her elbows on the table and rested her chin in her hands.

"Why did you throw it away?" Erin asked. "Maybe you can use it again."

"I felt sad about not going. I doubt if he'll ask me again since I'm so unreliable."

"Yeah," Erin teased, "I think he'll be really upset that you're obeying the Bible and your dad."

Tess gave her The Look out of the side of her eyes, but Erin smiled. "Anyway, I'll give Katie and Joann the invitations after lunch. They're in my backpack. Let's count the money."

They opened the envelope and sorted the bills into piles of ones, fives, and tens. Then Erin counted it.

"I think there's $250, not including yours and mine. How much did we need?"

"Two hundred and fifty dollars. So you don't have to pitch in," Tess said. "You're already both a junior bridesmaid and working at the shop."

"What about your ten dollars?"

"I'll buy the card or something," Tess answered.

"That's going to be one honking, large, happy card for ten

dollars," Erin said. "Hey, speaking of happy, did you see my brother last night?"

"Yeah," Tess said. "How come you didn't tell me they were going to hike?"

"I didn't know. My dad has Sundays and Mondays off now, so I guess they're hiking on Monday nights. How was I to know they would pick the same place as your dad?"

"Well," Tess said with a giggle, "I'm glad they did."

"I'll bet." Erin smiled. "And it's cool that everything else worked out all right. Do you think your dad thought more about Jesus after you talked?"

"No," Tess said. "But at least he's going to let me still go to church."

"I wish you weren't grounded though," Erin said. "I'm going to be totally bored if we can't talk on the phone every night."

"I know." Tess gulped. "But I'm more worried about Mr. Snodgrass's flipping out. And," she looked at her watch, "that's only four hours away."

thirteen

Mr. Crabgrass

Tuesday Afternoon, April 22

"I have the check right here." Tess patted her fanny pack in response to her mother's question.

"Well, make sure you give it to the florist right away. You don't want to lose it." Molly Thomas jerked the car into fourth gear and tore through the intersection just before the light turned red.

Erin glanced at Tess, a grain of fear in her eyes. Tess winked at her. "She's never crashed yet," she whispered.

"I don't want this to be the first time," Erin whispered back.

The traffic signals worked with them; they were almost all green on the short jaunt from home to the florist shop.

"You did ask Janelle if she was going to be there all day, right?" her mother asked, lips pursed. Her mom looked tired today.

"Yes. I called her this afternoon. She was on her way out the door, and she's staying till closing time. I called her right after I called Pastor Jack." Tess's cheer drooped.

"Oh. How did that go?" Erin asked.

"Okay, I guess. He was really disappointed I wouldn't be speaking. But he said he would ask Terri."

"Terri?" Erin said. "Oh, that's doubly bad."

"I know. But I guess I deserved it. And Jack doesn't know that Terri and I don't really get along." Terri was Melissa's best friend, but Terri was jealous every time Tess and Melissa worked together in the baby nursery. Tess remembered her own struggle with jealousy, which wasn't entirely resolved, and went pink.

"I'm sorry, Tess. But it could have been a lot worse." Her mother jammed the brakes on just in time to stop at a quickly turning yellow light. "Dad wanted to ground you from church altogether."

"I know. I feel better anyway with the truth out. More like myself." Tess smiled again.

"Just keep that in mind when you talk with Mr. Crabgrass," her mother said.

"Crabgrass!" Tess shouted. "Ha, Mom, that's perfect." Both girls practically laughed themselves out of their seat belts.

"What's so funny?" Her mother looked in the rearview mirror.

"His name. Didn't you make a joke? His name is Mr. Snodgrass, but you called him Mr. Crabgrass!" Tess burst out laughing again. And this time, her mother joined her.

"I guess it must have been a mental lapse," her mother admitted, still chuckling. "He's so crabby, it just seemed to fit."

"You've got that right!" Tess agreed.

"I think I have to go to the bathroom," Erin said, still giggling.

"Well, we're here. So, Mom, wait till I tell Mr. Crabgrass—I mean Mr. Snodgrass—before you abandon me," Tess said. "Thanks for the ride." She leaned forward to peck her mother on the cheek. "Stay in the parking lot till you see me wave. Just in case he throws me out of the store."

"I'll sit right here and watch through the window," her mother affirmed. "Be brave."

Tess walked inside to tell the truth.

As she opened the door, the cool air blasted out, but this time it wasn't as intimidating as before. Mr. Snodgrass was standing right up front, and there were no customers. Thank heaven. He was the type to yell no matter who was around.

"Hi, Mr. Snodgrass," Erin said first. "We're here to work."

"Well, it's about time," he answered. "I have a lot of prom orders to fill, and I could use you two to clean up the back. If you think you can." He sniffed.

"Here's the money." Tess offered him the check. Might as well start with the good news.

"Check?" he asked, lifting his glasses with one hand and scratching his eyelid with the other. "Check for what?"

"For our teacher's wedding flowers," Tess reminded him. "We collected cash from our class; then my mom wrote a check for it all."

"Oh. Hmm. Has she come in to order them?"

Tess looked at Erin, who looked back in distress. "She said she has," Tess answered.

"Well, then, I'm sure she did. I'll credit this to, to…," he stammered.

"Martinez," Tess offered.

"Yes. Martinez." He squinted, and Tess was not at all sure he knew who Ms. M. was.

"Well, get back there to work," he shouted. "Janelle is waiting for you."

"There's just one more thing," Tess said.

"What?" Mr. Snodgrass asked, looking at his watch.

"Well, Saturday you asked me if I had experience; I said yes, but I didn't tell you that my only experience is in my backyard, not at a shop or craft show or anything." Tess whooshed all the sentences out in one breath and cowered toward Erin, expecting him to erupt.

"I see." He grimaced. "Well, I don't suppose anything can be done about it now. I have your money, and I want you to clean up the back. All right, get on." He waved his hands impatiently. "I expect lots of hard work today and Thursday. No goofing off."

"About Thursday, Mr., um, Snodgrass," Tess's voice sounded little and squeaky even to her.

"More bad news, I suppose?"

"Well, I can come, but Erin can't."

Mr. Snodgrass started to sweat. "I guess I'll take what I can get. I have three proms to do flowers for, and I need the help." He grunted. "Now get back there with Janelle." He turned his back, but Tess heard him muttering about expecting anything decent from lazy kids these days.

Bitter acid rose in her throat, and she swallowed it quickly. Then she waved to her mother out the window, and her mom popped the Jeep into reverse.

"I can see why Janelle is quitting," Erin whispered to Tess as they headed to the workshop area. Tess nodded a big agreement.

"Hi, guys!" Janelle was a breath of warmth after that encounter.

"Hi," Erin answered. She and Tess tied on the aprons Janelle handed them.

"Lots to do today. See the bundles of wire over there?" She pointed at about a dozen piles of green florist wire.

"Yeah," Erin said.

"I need you to measure and snip the wire at three inches. They're for boutonnieres."

"What are those?" Erin asked.

"The little bouquets of flowers guys wear to the prom on their tuxedos."

"Cool! Do you have a date?" Tess asked.

"Yep, and I'm coming in Thursday to make his. And my corsage."

"Wow," Tess said. Both girls breathed out. It must be totally awesome to be a teenager. Tess, for one, could hardly wait.

She set to work snipping one of the stacks while Janelle sent Erin to clean a walk-in cooler. It felt good, using the heavy wire cutters to help ready the materials for someone's big night out. Not to mention Ms. M.'s Biggest Day of Her Life.

Thank you, Jesus, she prayed silently, *for not making Mr. Snodgrass wig out too badly and for not having him send me home. Thank you for using me to do something nice for lots of people.*

As soon as she finished one of the piles, Tess walked back to where Janelle worked. "Should I help Erin now?"

"Did you finish already?" Janelle asked.

"Yep!" Tess proudly pointed at her pile.

"Oh, Tess, you have to snip all the piles, not just one."

"Oh, sorry." She hadn't known Janelle meant to do them all. They must be making a lot of boutonnieres.

She started to snip again.

"Is your teacher psyched for her wedding?" Janelle asked.

"Totally," Tess answered. "That reminds me. Mr. Crabgrass—I mean, Mr. Snodgrass—wasn't sure he remembered Ms. Martinez, but she said she placed her order last week. I—uh—I'm afraid to ask him to check in his order box." She didn't tell Janelle why.

"Mr. Crabgrass! That's a good one!" She chuckled. "I'll check in a sec." Janelle finished arranging the carnations and went back toward the cooler.

"I hope your teacher did and that he already ordered the flowers," she called. "With all the proms and with Mother's Day in another week or so, the suppliers are running really low."

fourteen

Last Day

Thursday Afternoon, April 24

"Hi, Mr. Snodgrass." Tess ran into the shop and waved stiffly at the owner. He waved, too, but more to shoo her back to the workroom than as a hello.

Janelle already was hard at work, cutting foam florist blocks into squares.

"Did you find Ms. Martinez's order?" Tess asked, almost out of breath. Last Tuesday they had been unable to find it. Janelle said she would talk with Mr. Snodgrass about it.

"Yes, I found it," Janelle said. "It was filed under Rodriguez, her fiancé's name. I told you I'd call you if there was a problem," she reminded Tess. "Mr. Snodgrass misfiled it." She held out the paper to Tess.

Tess read the order. It included petals for tossing. No birdseed. She wondered if Erin knew.

"Whew, what a relief!" Tess slipped the order back into the file and bow-tied an apron behind her back. "I know you said you would call, but I thought, what if you forgot? And Ms. M. was raving today about how excited she was that she picked the flowers she wanted from the flower language book—whatever that means." Tess sat on the stool next to Janelle and carefully picked up a sharp-edged knife to cut the foam.

"Oh, some people think different flowers mean certain things. Like, baby's breath means 'ours is an everlasting love.' That's why so many people have it for their weddings." Janelle set aside the foam.

"Oh, yeah, Ms. M. told us she ordered baby's breath. And for all her bridesmaids she ordered bellflowers. What do they mean?"

Janelle walked over to a small book on the wooden table where the floral designer worked. "It means 'with gratitude.' So maybe she's thankful for their friendship."

"Awesome, can I see that book?" Tess thumbed through the pages. "What flowers are you getting for your date's boutonniere?"

"A pink rose, which means 'to my friend.' Because he's not really a boyfriend."

"Oh, cool. I wish I could give one of those to Erin," Tess said.

"Why don't you?" Janelle asked. "We could put together a little posy for her."

"Ooh. What's a posy?" Tess's eyes shone. This would be an amazing Secret Sister surprise.

"A posy is a little bouquet. You could use"—Janelle took the book from Tess and paged through it—"tiny pink geraniums, which mean 'our friendship is true.'"

Great! Tess dug in her pocket. She had some money from baby-sitting. She showed it to Janelle, who nodded.

"I'll make it for you in a minute. You can pay me, and when I go up front to work, I'll put it in the cash register."

Tess looked at the book for another minute. "Janelle, do we have any white chrysanthemums?"

"Uh, I think so. Why?"

"I want one for myself." Tess slipped back onto her stool. White chrysanthemums meant "I tell the truth." She would press it in her Bible.

"Okay." Janelle put together the little posy for Erin and stuck it in the back cooler with a single white chrysanthemum till it was time for Tess to go home. Tess handed her the money just as Mr. Snodgrass stormed into the back.

"Can you work up front now?" he asked Janelle. "I have to make some calls." He slammed the door behind him. Janelle winked at Tess and followed him.

A minute later he ran back into the workroom. "Don't just sit there!" he said to Tess, pointing at one of the ten or so stacks of floral foam. "Get cutting! Three-inch square pieces." Then he slammed out again.

Tess sat cutting, thinking about how great it was that Ms. M. chose the flowers she wanted, with the meanings she wanted—and how great it was that she was having flowers at all.

Jesus, I thought it was all up to me to make this plan work. I'm sorry I lied when I got scared things were going to blow up. Even though I was trying to be nice. Plus, God, you know where the Bible says that you can do more than we could ever ask or imagine? Well, what about Ms. M.'s honeymoon? I have no plan for that, which is probably a good thing, right? Ha-ha. Could you work something out for her your way? Thanks.

After praying, she felt expectant. Would God work out something without her?

Soon she finished her stack and timidly went up front. "I... I finished."

Mr. Snodgrass gave her a look of disbelief then walked back with her. "Do I have to spell it out for you?" he asked.

"Cut all the stacks of foam, not just one. I thought you would be smart enough to figure that out." Then he slammed the door behind him.

Tess hopped up on her stool again, trying to count her blessings: Ms. M.'s flowers, a cool posy for her Secret Sister, Tyler at church.

She let her mind wander, especially about Ms. M.'s wedding. What would she look like? What would the church be like? Would they write their own wedding vows? Tess wanted to, when she grew up and got married. About an hour and a half later, she had finished the stacks.

Nervous about confronting Mr. Snodgrass again, but even more nervous about having him walk in on her doing nothing, she tiptoed up front. "Um, excuse me," she said, walking up next to him. Janelle was helping a customer so she couldn't tell Tess what to do.

"What is it?" he asked. "I'm about to leave."

"Is there anything else I can do? I'll be here another hour or so." Tess hoped he would say, "No, go home." But he didn't.

"Yes." He walked her back to the roses' cooler. "See these?" He picked up one of seven or eight buckets on the shelves. Each held a different color of rose on long stems. As he shoved a bucket at her, the water slopped all over Tess's apron.

"I want you to cut them with two-inch stems for prom boutonnieres. Two inches. No more, no less." He held up two fingers as if he was talking to a baby. "Understand?" He tossed a ruler at her place on the worktable. Then he undid his own apron and started to walk toward the front. "Stick their stems in the stem trays with water and put them back in the cooler when you're done."

At least he was gone. Tess sat in her chair, humming, carefully slicing each bud off at two inches. She finished in just a few minutes. Then she walked back to get another bucket and put the empty one on the ground. Within an hour she had cut all the roses in the eight buckets. Time to go home.

She grabbed her posy and looked at the trays and trays of rosebuds. It seemed like an awful lot to her, all eight buckets. An awful lot. But, well, he was the boss. Maybe the designers were making hundreds and hundreds of boutonnieres. It seemed unlikely. But what did she know?

fifteen

Disaster

Friday Afternoon, April 25

The next school day passed quickly, because everyone was excited about the wedding. "Hey, we're supposed to get bathroom breaks every hour," Kenny called out to the substitute. "Otherwise Russell here will have an accident."

Russell elbowed him as the sub tried to maintain order in the class. Even Ms. M. found that almost impossible on a Friday. And today she was gone, getting ready for the wedding. Instead, this poor substitute had the thankless job of trying to keep order.

"You know what I heard?" Katie asked Tess, loudly enough for everyone to listen in. "I heard Ms. Martinez isn't coming back. Ever. In fact, I asked her myself yesterday, and she said it was true."

The entire class hushed. A piece of chalk rolled off the silver tray in front of the chalkboard and dropped to the ground, snapping in two. Nobody stepped forward to pick it up. Not even the sub. Katie liked to have fun, but she would never lie about something like that. Tess just stared, not answering.

"Katie, are you serious?" Joann asked. "Why didn't you tell me? I'm your very best friend and—" Joann clapped her hand over her mouth. Tess guessed she was about to say, "Secret Sister." She and Katie were Secret Sisters, too. But of course, that was a secret.

"I asked her, and she said that starting next week, our teacher would be Mrs. Rodriguez."

Oh, man. Ms. M. was leaving. And she hadn't even said good-bye!

"Katie, you goof," Tess realized with a laugh. "Ms. M.'s new name will be Mrs. Rodriguez!" The whole class exhaled its relief. Joann walked forward to put the chalk back on the tray, and the sub went to her desk.

"You're in big trouble, young lady," Kenny said in his most fatherly voice. "We'll get you back for this, wait and see. Maybe tomorrow at the wedding." The whole class giggled. Everyone looked forward to seeing the class's beloved teacher get married.

"You are *not* going to do anything to spoil that wedding," Erin said.

"Nope. I'll just get back at Katie," Kenny said. Practical jokes were his specialty. Erin waved him off, and she and Tess started to pick up their stuff to go home.

"I can't tell you how happy I am to be done working at that flower shop!" Tess said.

"Yeah, me, too," Erin said. "Thanks again for the posy." Tess had dropped it off at Erin's house last night.

"That was such a cool idea. I wish I had one of those flower books," Erin remarked.

"Me, too," Tess said. Then she told Erin about her prayer yesterday for the honeymoon.

"Do you think anything will happen?" Erin asked.

"I'm not sure," Tess answered. "But I'm hoping it will. Time's running out though. So I'm not really sure what God can do. I'm not interfering this time. No finagling to get my way. I think I've done just about enough finagling with the flowers."

"The flowers turned out fine, even after all the trouble," Erin reassured Tess. The final bell rang, and the class herded out the door.

"We had better get going," Tess said. "You have to get to bed early tonight so you're not tired for the big day. I wish I could call you tonight, but, you know."

"I know," Erin said. "But I'll see you tomorrow."

Tess took off down the street toward her house while Erin waited at the school for her mom to pick her up.

A few minutes later, Tess arrived at home. "Hi, Mom!" She opened the door and then shut it tightly, tossing her back-pack into a corner of the hallway and flipping off her shoes. Now for a little relaxation. A Coke, maybe. And a good book.

Her shoes landed smack in the center of the shoe basket. "Two points for me!" she cheered.

"Tess!" Her mother came running from the kitchen, drying her hands on a dishtowel. "I had an awful conversation with Mr. Snodgrass. He called first thing this morning and yelled practically nonstop for five minutes."

The blood emptied from Tess's face and slipped right past her heart to her feet. Mr. Crabgrass strikes again!

"What was the problem?" she asked.

"He claims he asked you to cut off the stems of one bucket of flowers, but you cut off eight buckets worth. Now they are a total loss. Is that true?"

"Oh, Mom, I'm dead." Tess sank to the floor right in the middle of the hallway. "I...I did do that. On Tuesday I only cut one wire bundle, and Janelle said, no, I was supposed to cut them all. Then yesterday I only cut one foam pile, and Mr. Snodgrass flipped out and told me to cut them all. So when he pointed to the buckets, well, I thought I was supposed to cut them all, too."

"Well." Her mother stood beside her, patting her shoulder. When Tess looked up, she couldn't even see her mom's face. Just her big, round belly.

Mom continued, "He wants us to come to the store as soon as you get home. I really don't know why. I suppose he'll want me to pay for them all." Her mother looked ready to cry.

Tess started to cry. "I'm sorry, Mom. I tried my best. That's really what he told me to do. Or what I thought. It did seem like a lot of roses, but he kept yelling at me every time I asked a question. So I didn't want to ask any more." She tried to calm down, but she couldn't help it. She ended up crying for a full five minutes.

"It will be okay, honey. Better go clean up a little," her mother said. "Tyler's at Big Al's today so we'll go to the shop just as soon as you're ready." Her voice shook a little.

Tess walked to the bathroom and splashed cold water on her face. *And I can't even talk to Erin.*

She felt a voice inside her say, *Talk to me.*

Yes, that was right.

"Jesus," she prayed, "this time I was trying really hard to do the right thing. Please help me survive this terrible disaster. I feel sick. Amen."

sixteen

Hopping Mad

Friday Afternoon, April 25

"How about I just stay in the car, and you go in?" Tess joked, trying to crack the tension.

"How about I stay in the car and you go in?" her mother said. Tess looked at her mom's face. It was straight.

"Are you serious?" Tess gulped. She supposed she would have to face it alone. It was her mistake, after all.

"No." Her mother leaned over and ruffled Tess's hair. "Would I leave you to face the Big Bad Wolf alone?" She unclasped her seat belt. "I'll come in with you."

"Thanks, Mom. Although I don't like being compared to the three little pigs." The two of them stepped out of the Jeep and into the hot spring day. It was at least ninety degrees out. Normal for Arizona, but today it seemed stuffy and especially hard for Tess to breathe.

The bells on the door tinkled as it opened, and Tess's mother let her go in first. Mr. Snodgrass eyeballed them but said nothing, finishing with his customer. His voice was sweet and thick as chilled honey, dripping with compliments. Tess knew the honey would sour to vinegar by the time he talked to her. She rubbed her hands over her forearms, trying to melt the goose bumps.

Finally, his customer left. "Well, I see you had the nerve to show up. I must say I'm surprised. It took a lot of gall to even come back after that little stunt."

"You did ask us to come in," Mrs. Thomas reminded him. "And I said we would."

"Come on in the back." Mr. Snodgrass shoved open the workroom door. "And see the mess you've made." He pointed at Tess, then stomped to the back door, which led to an alley. Pushing it open, he held it for them to walk through.

"See this? Boxes of useless roses. Nobody in town can use them; everyone's already ordered their own. I can't sell them all chopped up like that." He mopped his brow with the back of his hand.

"I'm really sorry," Tess said. "I thought you meant to cut them all."

"You thought? You could have fooled me. Anybody who was thinking would have known there were too many roses for boutonnieres. It's lucky for you, miss," he shook his finger in her face, "that my insurance covers this!"

Tess exhaled quietly, slowly, so Mr. Crabgrass couldn't see her relief. Her breath sounded like a tiny squirt of air escaping from a pinprick in a balloon. Her mom and dad wouldn't have to pay for this after all.

"I think you've harassed my daughter just about enough." Mrs. Thomas put her arm around Tess.

Tess drew in a breath. She needed to talk for herself. "I worked hard for you this last week, without pay. You didn't even have to take any money out of your own pocket to pay for my teacher's flowers. Your insurance paid for this. I worked really hard, and I don't deserve to be treated this way." She made sure her voice stayed respectful but strong.

Mr. Snodgrass said nothing.

"I think we're more than even. And we're leaving." Mrs. Thomas started to walk away. Tess pulled her shoulders back and raised her chin.

"If you're leaving, you can just take these boxes of dead rose heads with you. I don't ever want to see them, or you two, or talk with you again!" At that Mr. Snodgrass slammed the back door and went into his shop.

"Let's go," Tess's mother said. "You wait here, and I'll back up the Jeep so we can load the boxes. We'll throw them away at home."

A minute later she returned with the car, and after loading the boxes of withered rosebuds, they took off.

"I'm sorry this had to be your first experience with a job," her mom said.

Tess muttered, "Yeah." She felt responsible for the loss.

"Did I ever tell you about my first job?" her mom asked. "It was a disaster."

"Really?" Tess perked up.

"Yes. I worked at an ice-cream shop with another girl. I was in high school, and she and I were the only ones there at night. One night we noticed a car sitting in the parking lot, and a man was inside the car with a hat pulled low over his face. The car just sat there for hours, the man staring at us through the shop windows. Then he drove away. We were pretty scared, but we came back the next night, as usual."

Tess leaned closer to her mother.

"The next night he was there again. So I called my mom, your Grandma Kate, and asked her what to do. She said to call the police."

"And then what?" Tess held her breath.

"The police came. And guess who the man was?"

"Who?"

"My boss. He wanted to make sure we were working and not talking on the phone or eating ice cream. He was spying on us!"

"No way!" Tess burst out in giggles.

"Yes!" Her mom laughed. "We felt pretty dumb, but I'll bet he felt dumb, too, when he had to tell the police he was staking out his own shop."

"Maybe it was Mr. Snodgrass's father," Tess suggested. "Worst boss in training!"

"Maybe," her mother said, "but just remember, you do a good job because of who you are, not whether you like the boss!"

"I know," Tess said. "I tried to. At least Ms. M. will have flowers at her wedding. I can't wait to see them. I'll feel almost like I got them for her."

"You did, in a way." Her mom leaned over at a red light and kissed Tess's cheek. "You did really well, and I'm proud of you." She gunned the car at the first shade of green.

She said she was proud of me. Tess smiled, and the sun in her heart was at high noon again. And she could breathe just fine.

As they pulled into the garage, her mother said, "You know what? I have an idea. I know just what we can do with those droopy roses that will do good for someone else, too."

"What?" Tess asked. She opened the door to the house and walked in.

"I'll be right back." Her mother disappeared into her bedroom. Five minutes later she came dancing back into the kitchen.

"Mom, please, you'll fall and hurt the baby if you don't stop goofing around." *Talk about a dancing polar bear.* Good thing nobody else was home.

"I have wonderful news for you. Wonderful. This whole situation might turn out better than all right. And it involves Ms. Martinez."

"What is it?" Tess grabbed her mother's hands. "Tell me!"

"Okay," her mom said. "First, sit down."

Tess turned one of the kitchen chairs around and sat on it backward.

"Well, remember my friend who does potpourri?" her mother started.

"Yeah, the dried flower petals, right?"

"Yes. I called her to offer these rather than just throwing them away. And she was thrilled. Not only that, but she will pay you what she pays other suppliers, and that's good money."

"Pay me?" Tess leaped off her chair. "We can pay Mr. Snodgrass back then." She ran to get the phone and handed it to her mother. "Here, you dial."

Tess thumbed through the Scottsdale yellow pages until she found the shop. She read the number to her mother, and her mother dialed.

"Hello? Mr. Snodgrass?" she said. "This is Molly Thomas, Tess's mother. You know, we were just in your shop."

Tess's mom jerked the phone from her ear, holding it at least six inches away. Even Tess could hear Mr. Snod-grass holler, "I told you people I never wanted to hear from you again!"

"Well, I know, but see, we have some money—"

"Keep your money!" he shouted.

Tess heard a slam, and the line went dead.

"Well," her mother said, "he certainly has bad manners."

She stood up. "These chairs are hard on my back. Let's sit in the living room for a minute and decide what to do with that money."

Tess agreed and followed her mother. They cozied up on the couch next to a bookshelf.

"What can we do with it? I just don't feel right about keeping it ourselves," her mother said.

Tess nodded. As she thought about the excess money, she absent-mindedly scanned the shelf full of books. One title caught her eye, and she slipped the book into her lap. "*Hiking the Red Rocks of Sedona*," Tess read. "We haven't hiked there for a long time. Maybe after the baby comes."

"Isn't that where Ms. Martinez wanted to go for her honeymoon trip? Too bad that was cancelled."

Tess started to put the book back on the shelf. Then she stopped.

"Are you thinking what I'm thinking?" her mother spoke slowly, as their eyes met.

"Yes! But will it work? Is it too late?"

"I don't know. Get the phone book," her mother said.

Tess ran to the kitchen at top speed.

seventeen

Wedding Bells

Saturday, April 26

Tess's mother pulled up in front of the Spanish mission-style church just fifteen minutes before the wedding started.

"Do you have the card?" she asked.

"Yes." Tess stepped lightly out of the Jeep, thankful her mother hadn't ground the gears at this crucial moment.

"I'll see you afterward," her mom said.

"Okay." Tess waved, clutching the card, and walked toward the entrance.

The centuries-old church was a sculpted beauty, with dusky pink ceramic stucco smoothed over the graceful curves of southwestern architecture. Stocky palms lined the walkway to the front, and bottlebrush plants dropped their ruby blooms. Five bells, two stacked on two and one crowning the top, sat at the highest point of the church, ready to peal the best wedding wishes.

Tess noticed sweat from her hands had stained a corner of the card's envelope. Rats.

Just at the top of the walkway stood Erin. Tess picked up the pace to meet her. "Erin," she said, "you look beautiful!"

"Thanks." Erin giggled. Her watered silk dress was of the palest pink, like a streak of day in the evening sky. A bracelet of flowers circled her wrist. One of the fabulous ribbons from Mr. Snodgrass's shop trailed down the back of her head in curlicues.

"Couldn't have had this," Erin pointed at the flowers, "without you. And we have rose petals to toss at the end. Ms. M. used some of her flower money to buy them." Tess nodded, remembering the order slip.

Petals, petals everywhere, Tess thought. They were more than beautiful; they had power. Petal power. She clutched the card even tighter. She knew just what that petal power had purchased.

"Dreamy," Tess said with a sigh. "Are you going to sit by me, or do you need to be with the wedding party?"

"The wedding party is up front, remember?" Erin handed her a printed program. "I'll see you afterward though, okay?"

"Okay!" Tess took tiny, measured steps into the church.

Flickering candles lit the rows, and brass candleholders stood at stiff attention up the narrow aisle. The room was dim except for the candles and streams of color straining through the murky, stained-glass windows. Angelic strains of harp music washed through the room, accompanied by a sweet singing flute.

"Bride's side or groom's?" a tuxedoed man asked. He looked just like Ms. M. Maybe he was her brother.

"Bride's, please." He held out his arm and escorted Tess down the aisle, seating her across from Kenny and Russell.

As soon as her escort left, she leaned over. "What are you two doing on the groom's side? You don't even know the groom!"

"We're not sitting on any old girls' side, even if it's Ms. M.'s," Russell whispered back. "So there."

Tess turned and looked up front again but not for long. Someone bumped her elbow.

"Can we sit with you?" Katie asked.

"Of course." Tess let Katie and Joann scoot in front of her. She didn't let them have her spot though. She wanted to sit on the aisle so she could see Ms. M. when she walked down it.

"I hope she'll be happy," Joann said. Joann didn't believe in love.

"Of course she's happy!" Katie said. "And so will you be when we all come to your big wedding."

Joann frowned and bit her lip. Tess thought Joann was holding back a smile.

The groom appeared out of a door beside the altar and stood up front with his best man. Besides Erin, there was only a best man and a bridesmaid, Ms. M. had said. It would save them money.

"Ooh, he's gorgeous!" Katie whispered.

Tess nodded, and so did Joann. Underneath his black tuxedo were a golden-green silk vest and a matching Spanish tie. He smiled out at them. His smile was sweet and strong.

"Look how his hair waves back," Katie said. "So romantic. I knew Ms. M. would marry a handsome man." She swooned into Tess.

Tess agreed. Anthony—Mr. Rodriguez—was cute.

"Would you stop raving!" Joann whispered. "It's supposed to be quiet."

"I'll try," Katie said.

Just then the organist began to play. Everyone turned to look back at the door, where the bridesmaids stood.

Erin walked down the aisle first, holding her hands neatly by her side. Tess felt so proud. Even though Erin hated being in front of other people, she did just great.

The bridesmaid came next. Her dress was just like Erin's, only longer and with a little more trim. She held a modest bouquet tied together with a ribbon. Ms. M. had said her bridesmaid was her best friend.

"Will you be my bridesmaid when I get married?" Erin had asked Tess yesterday.

"Of course, silly. If you'll be mine," Tess had answered. She smiled now, remembering their conversation.

Then the organist began "The Wedding March." The entire church stood and looked back at Ms. M. and her dad at the top of the aisle.

Her dad was shorter than she was by just a little, but he stood tall and proud.

"Look at her!" Katie whispered.

Tess was looking, all right. The most beautiful bride in the world.

Ms. M.'s dress was a long waterfall of white silk and satin, with a trimmed bodice and off-the-shoulder sleeves. On her hands were delicate gloves the color of doves, a bow on the back of each one. And her veil! It cascaded all around her, hiding her face through a thin sheet of netting.

As she passed Tess, she lifted her bouquet ever so slightly, as if to say, "See what you girls provided?"

Thank you, Tess prayed. *Even when I messed it up, you straightened it out.*

The bouquet was a delicate blend of wedding roses and baby's breath, bachelor buttons, and a whole rainbow of other delicate blossoms that Tess didn't know the names of. And it wasn't any rinky-dink bouquet either. It was beautiful and huge. Mr. Snodgrass had come through after all. Two bouquets, petals, and Erin's headband. Not bad. He really did care about his work, like Janelle had said. Tess smiled.

Then Ms. M. reached the altar, and her father gave her to Mr. Rodriguez. The girls sighed and sat down.

The vows were said, and half an hour later, the groom lifted Ms. M.'s veil to kiss his bride.

The organist played another tune, this one quick, lively, and cheery, as the new Mr. and Mrs. Rodriguez marched back down the aisle together. It was time for the reception.

And only Tess knew what a huge surprise awaited them there.

eighteen

Red Rocks

Saturday, April 26

Once outside, the newlyweds stood to the side to receive people as they passed by to shake hands, kiss their cheeks, or wipe away a happy tear. As the guests reached the end of the line, Erin gave them a little handful of rose petals from her basket.

The bride and groom waited for their guests to line the sidewalk under a twig-covered arbor. Then the couple walked down the sidewalk between all of the guests. Showers of petals fluttered over the two, as they passed by the guests. The petals clung to their teacher's veil and to the groom's tux as they laughed and led the way to the nearby reception room.

"I couldn't call you because I'm grounded from the phone," Tess said to Erin, "and we didn't have time before the wedding. But something really terrible happened, then God turned it into something great."

In the time it took to walk into the reception room, Tess told Erin the whole story.

"That is so amazing! She'll be shocked when she opens that card."

Mr. and Mrs. Rodriguez cut into their ivory-frosted wedding cake. Bride and groom teddy bears perched on top.

"How cute!" Katie said.

Joann rolled her eyes.

After the girls collected some punch and cake, they sat down to dig in.

"Hey, something's on your back," Joann said to Katie.

"What is it? Get it!" Katie said.

Tess moved away from her. Maybe it was a bug.

Joann peeled a sticker off Katie's dress. It said, "Kiss me, I'm crazy."

"Ooh, that Kenny," Katie said. "He promised he would get me back." She giggled. "I guess he did."

"Shh," Joann said. "Ms. M.'s opening the cards."

Within a few minutes, their teacher opened the card from the class.

"What…what is this?" she asked, holding a check in her hands.

"It's a check. For your honeymoon," Tess said as she stood up. There sure were a lot of people in the room.

"How did you get this?" the new Mrs. Rodriguez asked.

"I…I'll tell you later," Tess said. She didn't want to explain to the whole room about making a mistake with the flowers.

"I'll bet it involves crime," Kenny said.

Russell and a few other boys laughed.

"No, it doesn't," Erin defended.

Mrs. Rodriguez walked over to their table and bent low to talk with them. "Thank you, girls, but I've already cancelled the reservations. And this wouldn't be enough." She spoke tenderly and blushed, near tears.

"Yes, it is," Tess told her. "When we got this money, my mom called around to different Red Rocks resorts in

Sedona until she found the one that had your reservation last week. Then she explained about your gift to your niece, and about this money."

She took a deep breath before continuing. "They thought it was great you were helping Amber. So they said if you brought this check, they would cover the rest for two nights."

"Thank you, thank you, girls." Ms. M.—or rather, Mrs. Rodriguez—really did have tears in her eyes now. "You are all so wonderful I don't know what to say."

"Say we have no tests for the rest of the year!" Russell suggested, and a great cheer went up. They all laughed, and just then a small mariachi band started to play Mexican music.

An hour or so later, Tess and Erin said their good-byes and went outside to wait for Tess's mom.

"Wasn't it a dreamy wedding?" Tess asked.

"Yep. It sure was." Erin took off her floral wristband. "Here, I want you to have this. It'll look really neat when the flowers dry, and you can hang it on your wall."

"Thanks," Tess said. She put it on. "I won't be visiting a flower shop for a while." She giggled, and Erin giggled with her.

Tess scooped up a handful of petals from the grass and let them flutter to the ground. They floated freely. Hey, she was free, too. The truth had set her free. She hadn't needed to lie; she never needed to lie. She needed to do the right thing and leave the details to the One who could handle them.

"Amazing what these little petals can do. Petal power! Who knew they could buy a honeymoon?" Tess said.

"Who knew?" Erin agreed.

"God did." Tess smiled.

"Yeah, God did," Erin agreed. "Even when we can't change things, he takes care of things best."

Just then Tess's mother screeched into the parking lot and slammed the brakes on right in front of them. She smiled as she unlocked the doors.

"And some things," Tess whispered, "never change!"

Have More Fun!!

Visit the official website at:
www.secretsisters.com

There are lots of activities, exciting contests, and a
chance for YOU to tell me what you'd like to see in
future Secret Sisters books! AND—be the first to know
when the next Secret Sisters book will be at your book-
store by signing up for the instant e-mail update list. See
you there today!

If you don't have access to the Internet, please write
to me at:

Sandra Byrd
P.O. Box 2115
Gresham, OR 97030

Language of Flowers

Tess gave Erin a cool posy full of Secret Sisters sentiments. Want to make one for your Secret Sister or maybe your mother or grandmother? Pick a bouquet, or if you can't find real flowers, break out the colored pencils and sketch some. Here are the meanings of a few flowers to get you started:

Amaryllis—pride
Apple blossoms—preference
Bluebells—constancy
Chrysanthemums (red)—love
Chrysanthemums (white)—truth
Clover—think of me
Crocus—happiness
Daffodil—regard
Daisy—innocence
Geranium—true friendship
Honeysuckle—generous affection
Iris—message
Lily of the valley—return of happiness
Marigold—sadness
Orange blossoms—purity and loveliness
Periwinkle—early friendship
Rhubarb—advice
Rosebud (white)—girlhood
Garland of roses—reward of virtue
Tulip—fame
Violet—faithfulness

From the *Language of Flowers* by Kate Greenway

What to do when you've finished this book? Solve these clues to the S.S. Handbook!

Across

2 A bunch of friends getting together to have a good time

3 Having a great time is having _____.

4 As teddies, they're cuddly.

8 Stirring up ingredients for lots of yummy fun

9 We'll stick to your refrigerator to remind you of important things.

11 Slumber party

Down

1 With glitter and glue and paper and fun, you've got something to keep when the two of you are done.

4 Stick us in your books, and we promise to hold your place.

5 In order to spend me, you gotta earn me first.

6 When you have good friends and something fun to do, you want to do it _____.

7 Doing something for others to show them how much you care

10 Drawing, painting, sketching, design

Look for the Other Titles in
Sandra Byrd's Secret Sisters Series!
Available at your local Christian bookstore

Available Now:

#1 *Heart to Heart:* When the exclusive Coronado Club invites Tess Thomas to join, she thinks she'll do anything to belong—until she finds out just how much is required.

#2 *Twenty-One Ponies:* There are plenty of surprises—and problems—in store for Tess. But a Native American tale teaches her just how much God loves her.

#3 *Star Light:* Tess's mother becomes seriously ill, and Tess's new faith is tested. Can she trust God with the big things as well as the small?

#4 *Accidental Angel:* Tess and Erin have great plans for their craft-fair earnings. But after their first big fight will they still want to spend it together? And how does Tess become the "accidental" angel?

#5 *Double Dare:* A game of "truth or dare" leaves Tess feeling like she doesn't measure up. Will making the gymnastics team prove she can excel?

#6 *War Paint:* Tess must choose between running for Miss Coronado and entering the school mural painting contest with Erin. There are big opportunities—and a big blowout with the Coronado Club.

#7 *Holiday Hero:* This could be the best Spring Break ever—or the worst. Tess's brother, Tyler, is saved from disaster, but can the sisters rescue themselves from even bigger problems?

#8 *Petal Power:* Ms. Martinez is the most beautiful bride in the world, and the sisters are there to help her get married. When trouble strikes her honeymoon plans, Tess and Erin must find a way to help save them.

The Secret Sister Handbook: 101 Cool Ideas for You and Your Best Friend! It's fun to read about Tess and Erin and just as fun to do things with your own Secret Sister! This book is jam-packed with great things for you to do together all year long.